MORE TALES TO KEEP YOU UP AT NIGHT

MORE TALES TO KEEP YOU UP AT NIGHT

BY DAN POBLOCKI
ILLUSTRATED BY MARIE BERGERON

Penguin Workshop

PENGUIN WORKSHOP
An imprint of Penguin Random House LLC, New York

First published in the United States of America by Penguin Workshop, an imprint of Penguin Random House LLC, New York, 2023

Text copyright © 2023 by Dan Poblocki
Illustrations copyright © 2023 by Penguin Random House LLC

Photo credits: i: AlexandrBognat/iStock/Getty Images, klyaksun/iStock/Getty Images; vii: DutchScenery/iStock/Getty Images; 13, 133, 183: alenkadr/iStock/Getty Images.

Penguin supports copyright. Copyright fuels creativity, encourages diverse voices, promotes free speech, and creates a vibrant culture. Thank you for buying an authorized edition of this book and for complying with copyright laws by not reproducing, scanning, or distributing any part of it in any form without permission. You are supporting writers and allowing Penguin to continue to publish books for every reader.

PENGUIN is a registered trademark and PENGUIN WORKSHOP is a trademark of Penguin Books Ltd, and the W colophon is a registered trademark of Penguin Random House LLC.

Visit us online at penguinrandomhouse.com.

Library of Congress Cataloging-in-Publication Data is available.

Printed in the United States of America

ISBN 9780593387504

1st Printing

LSCC

Design by Mary Claire Cruz

This book is a work of fiction. Any references to historical events, real people, or real places are used fictitiously. Other names, characters, places, and events are products of the author's imagination, and any resemblance to actual events or places or persons, living or dead, is entirely coincidental.

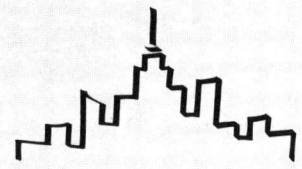

**For Lilith, again,
with even more love and gratitude—DP**

TRACKLIST

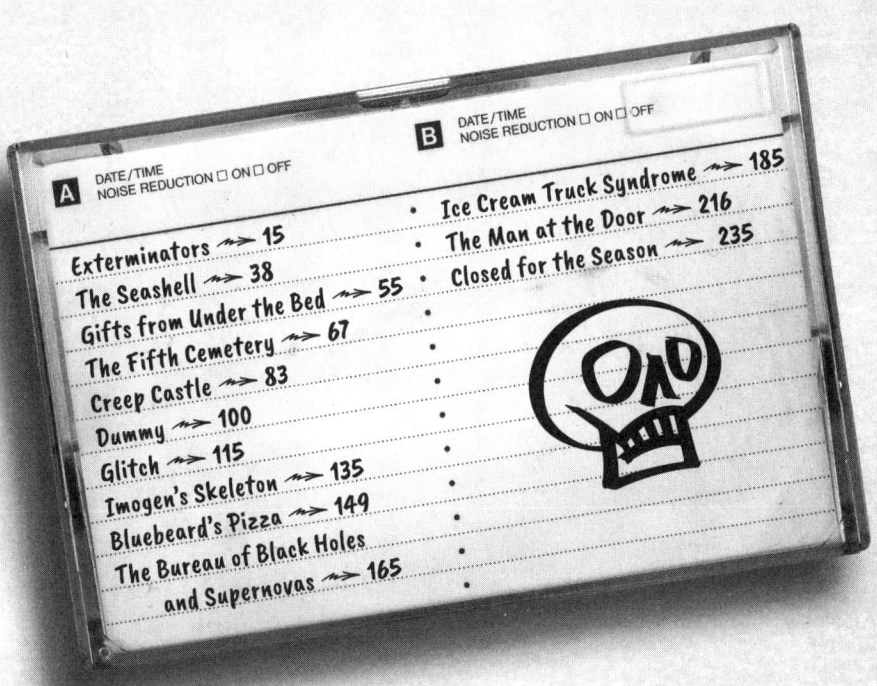

A
- Exterminators → 15
- The Seashell → 38
- Gifts from Under the Bed → 55
- The Fifth Cemetery → 67
- Creep Castle → 83
- Dummy → 100
- Glitch → 115
- Imogen's Skeleton → 135
- Bluebeard's Pizza → 149
- The Bureau of Black Holes and Supernovas → 165

B
- Ice Cream Truck Syndrome → 185
- The Man at the Door → 216
- Closed for the Season → 235

GILBERT GETS A CALL

Gilbert Campbell was shelving books at the public library on the Upper West Side when his phone dinged. One new voicemail.

His brother's message was garbled, mixed with static, but Gilbert was able to make out: *". . . tell you . . . Important . . . Whatever you do . . . Don't listen to the tapes . . . Explain more when I . . ."*

This was followed by about thirty seconds of a soft hissing.

Gilbert played the message again.

Then again.

Was there panic in Ant's voice? Or did it only sound that way because the recording was messed up?

It was the week of winter break. Holiday festivities had come and gone. Gilbert and his best friend, Percy, had been planning on playing video games and catching up on their favorite shows, but he hadn't thought to ask Mrs. Effiong for time off—a bummer, especially since this particular library was up by their school and nowhere near home. His mom and dad were away on vacation, and Grandma Rosemary was visiting. This wasn't a bad thing—Grandma Rosemary didn't mind TV bingeing or video games. In fact, she often joined in. The problem was that whenever their grandmother looked after them, Gilbert's older brother tended to act out.

Whatever you do . . . Don't listen to the tapes, Ant had said.

Which tapes? Gilbert wondered.

Before returning the call, he noticed that Ant's message was from early that morning—before dawn—but it had only just arrived.

Weird.

The line rang and rang.

Shivering, he returned to the shelving cart, deciding to grill Ant later. Since his shift was nearly done, only three books were left: *The Secret of the Stone Child* by Nathaniel Olmstead, *The Clue of the Incomplete Corpse* by Ogden Kentwall, and something called *Elsewhere Gardens* by an author named October Bowen.

This last one he handed to Mrs. Effiong across the counter. "I'd like to check this out before I go. It's for my best friend." Percy was a self-proclaimed botanist-in-training. Once, they'd said, *What in the world is more hopeful than a garden?* Gilbert loved that. Mrs. Effiong's big brown eyes glinted as she scanned the copy into his account.

Gilbert's phone dinged again—a message from Percy.

Their ears must be burning!

> My mom wants to know if you can come over for pizza later.

Gilbert typed back:

> Sure! I'd love to have pizza with your mom. Will you be there too?

> HAR. HAR.

Mrs. Effiong tsked as she slid the book to him. "Gilbert, you know I don't like our volunteers on their phones—"

"I just have to check in with my grandmother. I'll be quick."

When Gilbert pulled up Grandma Rosemary's contact info, the phone buzzed in his hand. She was calling! Ignoring Mrs. Effiong's frown, he swiped to answer, to say something about the cheerful coincidence. But his grandma sounded frantic. "Where have you been? I've called and called!"

"Service is spotty at the library. What's wrong?"

"It's Antonio."

His brother's strange voicemail crackled through Gilbert's memory. "Is he okay?"

"Do I *sound* like he's okay?" Grandma Rosemary sighed. "I'm sorry, sweetheart. It's just . . . he got hurt."

"How hurt?"

"We're in intensive care. Please come." She told him the hospital name. "The entrance is by the river."

A map of the city flashed through his frazzled mind. "I'll catch the bus."

"I have to get in touch with your parents—"

There was a click. She'd hung up.

"Everything all right?" Mrs. Effiong asked.

Gilbert felt like he was floating. His skin had gone all prickly. He thought of Ant's face—his bulbous nose, stubborn acne, dark fuzz on his chin, curly black hair that faded to the skin just over his ears. Then, Gilbert's brain did a frightening thing—it covered Ant's face in red.

Wet and sticky.

Like in horror movies.

"Gilbert?" Mrs. Effiong's voice came again. "What's the matter?"

Gilbert clutched the counter's edge, then slipped Percy's botanical book under his arm. "My brother . . . There was an accident. I—I have to go."

Mrs. Effiong's hand drifted toward her mouth. "Is there someone I can call?"

"My grandmother wants me at the hospital." Gilbert's voice sounded as if it belonged to someone else. "And my parents are—"

"Let me give you cash for a cab."

"I have a MetroCard."

"I'm not sure I feel comfortable—"

"I'll be fine. Promise." He retrieved his coat and scarf and hat from the chair behind the circulation desk.

"You have my cell number?" the librarian asked.

Strange how those were the words that should make his eyes sting. "I do," he answered, fighting to look *all business*.

"Text me when you get where you're going?"

An accident . . .

Intensive care . . .

Big brother . . .

He shook the thoughts away, then tossed a nod to Mrs. Effiong. If he stood there any longer, he knew he'd break. At the landing, he pushed the door open.

Cold air rushed into the library like a gasp.

Snow flurries started when the crosstown bus finally stopped.

Gilbert tugged his scarf tight and trudged to the hospital entrance around the corner. A security guard pointed him to the second floor. Upstairs, Gilbert stepped into a busy corridor. His phone chimed with a new message from Percy.

My mom wants to know what toppings you want? Meatballs? Peppers? Olives?

Percy! In the rush to get here, Gilbert had forgotten to tell them about Ant's accident.

> My brother's in the hospital.

> OMG. Everything all right?

> I'll text you in a bit.

Percy answered with a bunch of question marks. Gilbert was filled with a bunch of question marks himself.

He remembered to text Mrs. Effiong, then crept to the room the security guard had mentioned.

The door was open wide. Inside, a dim light hung on the wall over a headboard. A large silhouette was standing between Gilbert and the room's occupant. A nurse? A doctor?

Gilbert knocked. "Hello?"

The figure straightened, then bolted to a hidden corner of the room. Startled, Gilbert grabbed at the door frame and nearly dropped the library book for Percy that he realized he was somehow still holding on to.

Finally, he saw his brother, and any notion of the shadowed figure flew out of his head.

Tubes and hoses and bags filled with clear liquids hung from hooked stands on either side of the bed where Ant was lying. His eyes were closed. An oxygen mask covered his nose and mouth.

Gilbert took Ant's hand. "Wh-what happened to you?"

A noise came from behind him. He turned to find a closed door. *That shadowed figure . . . Was this where they'd gone?* A small placard read RESTROOM.

He looked to his brother. A large bandage covered Ant's lower left cheek. Another was taped to Ant's throat, snaking beneath his hospital gown. The skin around Ant's eyes was purple with collected blood.

The noise came again. Fabric rustling? Wind through air vents? Wings fluttering? "Who's there?" Gilbert asked.

When no answer came, his hope that the person was a nurse or doctor—or even his grandmother—evaporated.

Nervous, Gilbert glanced around for something to block the door. The wood-framed chairs in the corner wouldn't be heavy enough. Then the latch clicked, and the bathroom door opened a crack. A sliver of black. Gilbert sidled against the wall beside the door, out of the sightline, and listened to the nothingness within. A moment later, he clasped the library book like a baseball bat, yanked the doorknob, and shouted, "*Hyah!*"

A toilet was against the far wall, a chrome handle attached to the tiles, a corner sink stuck beside a cramped shower stall.

No one was there.

He looked to Ant with a nervous grin. Had he really shouted *hyah*? "You'd better not remember that," he whispered.

He flicked the bathroom light switch. In the shower stall, a leather satchel sat, sagging in on itself. Curious, Gilbert flipped it open. Inside, a few objects glinted. Plastic. Angular. He held one of them to the light.

At first, he wasn't sure what to make of it. A rectangular thing no bigger than his own hand. Then, his mind was whipped back to the garbled words of his brother's voicemail. *Don't listen to the tapes.* These were cassettes—tapes like the ones Grandma Rosemary kept in a box in a cupboard in her living room, next to an old boom box. Gilbert upended the satchel onto the floor. Two more cassette cases clattered out, followed by something larger, heavier. The player was bright yellow. *Walkman* and *AM/FM* were stenciled onto its side. A set of headphones slipped out too, attached to the player by a thin black cord. Totally retro.

Did the bag belong to Ant?

Footsteps echoed from the hallway. Gilbert shoved the bag's contents back inside, along with the library book. He turned off the bathroom light, then stared out through the crack in the door. The person who appeared was small. She placed a paper bag on the table beside the hospital bed, let out a sigh, then ran a hand across her short, graying hair.

Clutching the satchel's straps, Gilbert elbowed the door open and said, "Hi, Grandma . . ."

She startled. "Oh, honey. You scared me!"

Something told him to not show her his discovery, so when she hugged him briefly, he dropped the satchel and nudged it under the bed.

Her eyes were pinkish. "I grabbed us some coffees."

Gilbert took the cup even though he didn't drink coffee. He glanced at his brother again, all of his worry rushing back. "What happened?"

Here's what Grandma Rosemary told him:

That morning before work, she'd noticed Ant's door open, his bed made. Antonio's absence didn't surprise her. He'd often crash at a friend's place if it got late and he was sleepy. But when Ant didn't answer his phone, she'd fretted. She almost woke Gilbert but hadn't wanted to worry him. Then, at her office, she reached out to some of Ant's friends . . . By noon, she'd begun contacting emergency rooms.

Someone had found Ant on a subway platform sometime before sunrise.

He'd been unconscious from the start, his skin marked with strange wounds, deep gouges and scrapes. The IVs now connected to his arm were filled with antibiotics and saline and some medication for pain.

As soon as Grandma Rosemary took a breath, Gilbert asked, "Did you get in touch with Mom and Dad?"

"They're booking a flight back."

"Is he going to be okay?"

"The medicine will do what it's supposed to." There was something in Grandma Rosemary's voice that felt like a lie.

Together, they held Ant's hand. Gilbert felt Ant's pulse just below the skin under his knuckles. Faint. He thought again of the voicemail his brother had left him. About the tapes. What else had it said?

Ant had been keeping secrets. That much was clear, and it wasn't only the past twelve hours that proved it. In the weeks leading up to the holiday, Ant had been acting funny. Quiet. Tired. Even his friends had called him out on it. Last week, Fernando and Rosalie had stopped by, and Gilbert could have cut the tension between them with a laser beam.

Unfortunately, most warning signs are recognizable only in retrospect.

"What now?" he asked.

"We wait," she said, reaching for her coffee.

That was one thing Gilbert was not willing to do.

In the hospital cafeteria, he bought a chocolate chip cookie and a small bottle of apple juice. When his phone chimed yet again, he ducked toward a secluded table near the tall windows.

Any news?

But Gilbert didn't want a whole back-and-forth just yet.

Instead, he stacked the cassettes on the table. The labels read *More Tales to Keep You Up at Night*, and each was numbered. *One, Two, Three.*

Don't listen to the tapes . . .

Gilbert opened his voicemail app and played the garbled message again. Clearly, *these* were the tapes. He thought of Ant—stubborn and silly and oftentimes rude—and then banged his fists on the table. The stack rattled.

How could you ask someone to *not* listen to something, then leave that very thing for them to find?

But his brother had been unconscious when they'd brought him here.

Which meant . . . what?

That the dark figure at Ant's bedside had really been there?

That they'd left the satchel for Gilbert?

If so, didn't that mean he *should* heed Ant's voicemail warning?

He took a deep swig of apple juice.

Ant had mentioned the tapes in his last bit of communication. That had to mean something.

Gilbert needed to figure out what that something was.

Unlike the earbuds Gilbert was used to, the Walkman's phones had wide foam pads that hugged his head like muffs for cold weather. He popped open the player, reached for the tape marked *One,* fit it inside, then closed the Walkman's lid. When he pressed PLAY, a warm, not unpleasant voice—expressive and musical, masculine with a hint of rasp—began to speak, as if directly to him.

EXTERMINATORS

First, you should know that Tony wasn't tall, wasn't broad. Also, his nose was wide, and his teeth were slightly crooked, and his eyebrows had started to join in the middle. He didn't have a problem with how he looked, but other boys in gym class made him feel like a troll.

When he tried to stand up to them one afternoon, they ganged up on him. That is, until Matt Miller—six foot two, thick as a slab, and growing still—stepped in, put them in their places. The details of how it went down aren't necessary. If you've ever been young, you know the story.

Tony was a freshman that year. Matt was two years older.

After school, Tony found Matt waiting for him on the wide front staircase leading down to the sidewalk on Seventh Avenue. Students stepped around him. Matt was a boulder in a stream, and the others were rushing water. Matt smiled and waved Tony over. Tony almost got swept up in the crowd, but Matt pulled him aside. "You okay?" he asked.

Tony hated that his face was getting warm. "I can handle those guys."

"Yeah, I know. It's just . . . some of them live on my block, so they listen to me more than other people."

Tony's cheeks were burning now. "Oh. Well. Thanks."

"What are you up to?"

"Right now?"

Tony played off his nerves as best he could, kept quiet, let Matt do most of the talking. They went down the block to the chocolate shop, and Matt bought Tony a mocha latte. They sat at the corner table in the back.

That first day was just for fun. A getting-to-know-you kind of thing. Like: "Maybe let's be friends." Tony learned that Matt had two older sisters. Both were in community colleges out of the city, hoping to transfer to bigger schools after their sophomore years. Money was tough. Matt's parents were city employees, though Matt never said doing what. Tony shared that he had a younger brother, his parents worked for non-profits, his grandmother lived across the city with her sister, his great-aunt, that they'd traveled together from St. Croix when they were young, following other family members who'd come before them. The boys talked about video games and their neighborhoods and comic books. Turned out they liked the same titles. When they finished their drinks, they strolled to the local comics shop and wandered the aisles. By the time Tony made it home, he felt different.

It had never been easy for him to connect with people.

In conclusion: Matt Miller was cool.

They went on like that for a long while. Making jokes through phys ed class. Grabbing coffees after school. Stopping by the comics store. Heading to the park to read and talk about how they'd change some of the stories if they could.

A month into the following school year, Matt asked Tony if he wanted to make some extra cash. Matt was having trouble keeping up with a new job and needed a break.

Of course, Tony wanted to help. "It's not anything illegal, is it?"

"Not that I know of."

"What do I have to do?"

The gig sounded easy enough: Pick up an envelope. Drop off the envelope. Get paid.

"Why don't they just *mail* the envelopes?"

"They need them faster than that. Like . . . a messenger service."

"That would be us?"

"Exactly. *Messengers*."

"What's in the envelopes?" Tony asked.

At this, Matt's expression grew darker. "That's not our business. The boss has a bunch of rules. It's best to not break them."

Tony shrugged. "Shouldn't be a problem," he replied, though he felt unsure now whether he wanted to get involved at all. "I can follow rules."

Matt raised an eyebrow. "Rule one: Knock on the boss's door three times only. Two: Never look inside the envelope. Three: Take the subway directly to the office. Four: Get your cash and go home." Matt pulled a leather satchel from under his chair and plopped it on the table between them. "One more thing." Tony peeked inside. "The boss needs you to listen to these tapes before you can start."

"Really? What for?"

"He said they give you access. To his building, I guess? I'm not sure why, but I listened to them too." Matt reached into the bag and removed an old Walkman AM/FM radio cassette player. "Think you can get through these tonight?"

Tony listened. The tapes weren't filled with music, as he'd been expecting, but with a voice telling a bunch of scary stories. There were tales of curses and revenge. Stories of doors—portals to other places—where inhuman creatures could cross into our world. Stories of the search for forbidden knowledge. There was even a story about where the tapes had come from.

After he'd finished, Tony noticed an odd sensation in his chest. He felt changed somehow, as if he knew more about his universe now and his place in it. Yet, the feeling didn't *bother* him. He knew that stories have power.

Could this be what Matt had meant by *access*? When Tony asked him at school the next day, Matt shrugged. He gave Tony the addresses where he'd pick up and drop off the envelopes.

"How often do I do this?"

Matt wouldn't meet his gaze. "Every day."

A shiver crept across Tony's skin. "For how long?"

"Not long. Like I said before, I just need a little break is all."

The brick building was easy enough to find. Almost directly at the top of the subway steps. The entryway was through an iron gate, across an overgrown evergreen garden. The empty lobby's marble floor was mostly black, with flecks of gold that caught what little light came in through the doorway. At the elevator, Tony caught an acrid whiff and saw the flickering light overhead, so he took the stairs instead. Five flights were enough to steal his breath.

His parents would certainly ground him for even *thinking* about doing this. All he'd told them was that he'd joined a new club after school and he'd be coming home later than usual.

The door was at the far end of the dull beige hall. Staring at the peephole, Tony was overcome with a sudden fear. As if whoever lived here was watching him. Remembering Matt's rules, Tony knocked. Three times. A plain white envelope emerged from the bottom of the door. He picked it up, turned around, walked quietly back down the silent stairs.

The train arrived as Tony made it to the platform. He knew the subway routes like the backs of his hands. If he stayed on this train (no transfer), he'd make it to the destination in about an hour. He settled into the seat, patted the pocket of his jacket where he'd stuck the envelope, then pulled his homework from his knapsack. He made it through all of geometry and half of his history chapter before arriving at the station.

In the brisk evening air, the surroundings belonged to a different city—wide lots with cracked asphalt, brown grass grown up tall in patches, an emptiness that felt opposite from his own neighborhood. A salty tang coated his tongue. Docks stretched out past a tall chain-link fence. Lights from a few houseboats glowed upon the black water. A horn sounded—a passing ship signaling danger off the coast.

A warehouse stood about a block away. The entry was illuminated by a dim sconce under which was a diamond-shaped sign reading EMBER'S EXTERMINATORS. Tony tried the knob, but it was locked. There was a mail slot in the middle of the door. He knocked, three times, like at the apartment. To his surprise, a voice spoke from the other side, "Go 'head." Then, as if flicked by fingers, the mail slot's cover rattled.

Tony shoved the envelope inside. A moment later, a small package popped out of the slot and fell to the ground—a yellowish envelope, a thick stack of bills inside. "Is this all for me?" he asked, but the voice did not come again.

An hour or so later, Tony was home.

During the journey, he'd tried to make himself look as

small as possible, which wasn't hard, since he was already pretty small. The yellow envelope weighed heavy in his pocket. There'd been no taxis near the docks.

Tony called Matt Miller from his bedroom.

"Hello?" Matt sounded like he'd been sleeping.

"You all right?"

"Just tired. You?"

Tony hesitated. "I did the thing."

"Worked okay?"

"I think so. It's just . . . this isn't what I was expecting."

Matt scoffed. "Not enough?"

Tony laughed, surprised. "More than enough."

"Is there a problem?"

"Do you . . . want half?"

"*No*," Matt answered quickly. A moment of quiet. Then, he added, "It's all yours, bud."

The next day, Matt barely looked at Tony during gym class. Afterward, when Tony tried to ask him what was wrong, he shrugged and walked away. Maybe he *was* angry about the money, after all?

After school, Tony caught the train. Picked up the envelope. Dropped it at the warehouse.

He hid the cash in his bedroom.

Over the next few weeks, Matt continued to give Tony the

cold shoulder. Tony felt so frustrated, he almost said he didn't want to do the job anymore. There was so much money in his bedside table, it seemed almost pointless to collect more. Tony might have actually quit, but he worried Matt might never speak to him again.

But then, about a month after Matt had asked him to take over the deliveries, he stopped showing up at school. Tony called a few times to check in. Matt's parents said he wasn't feeling well or that he was asleep.

Finally, one evening, Matt answered the phone himself. "You've got to stop calling," he said quietly, quickly.

"Why?"

"It's too much."

Tony pressed. "Are you sick? Everyone is worried about you."

"Everyone?" A punch in the chest. Matt meant: *You?*

"What's going on?"

Matt Miller was silent for several seconds. "Maybe we shouldn't talk anymore."

This hurt even more. "I don't get it."

"You don't need to get it. In fact, it's *best* if you don't get it."

"What about the job?"

"Keep it." Tony had to sit on the floor to keep the world from going dark. "Follow the rules and you'll be fine."

Something occurred to him, and he asked quickly, "Did *you* follow the rules?" The line went still. After a few seconds, a signal rang in his ear. When Tony tried calling back, there was no answer.

School the next day felt like walking through molasses. Whatever was going on was because of the job. But why? What could have happened? Tony thought of the last thing he'd said to his friend: *Did you follow the rules?*

That afternoon, when he reached the boss's door, Tony hesitated before knocking. He reached for the knob, as if to turn it, maybe even walk inside, confront the person behind all this. But his gut squelched, insisting that would be a huge mistake. What if he asked a few questions? To help Matt? That too felt like the wrong idea. So he knocked. Three times. A moment later, as always, the white envelope appeared at his feet. Tony snatched it up and ran.

Minutes later, in his usual spot in the corner of the train car, Tony glared at the envelope. Maybe the answer to what was going on with Matt was hidden inside. Without thinking, Tony held it up to the dingy fluorescent light. The outline of a ragged scrap of paper appeared, marked with the hint of dim scribbles. He squinted, and the backlit writing became clear. Trembling, Tony shoved the envelope into his pocket, where it should have been in the first place, then climbed down and pushed himself against the plastic seat, hoping no one had seen.

The words in the envelope had been a name, scrawled in dark ink: *Matt Miller.*

When Tony reached the exterminator's office, he slipped

the envelope through the mail slot, then walked away, ignoring the package that dropped to the sidewalk behind him.

That night, Tony had trouble falling asleep. He couldn't stop thinking about the twisted tapes that Matt Miller had asked him to listen to. The stories had rooted into his mind. Every time he glanced at the clock on his nightstand, it felt like only a few minutes had crept by. Just before dawn, he began to dream.

There was a knocking. Someone at the front door of the apartment. He turned over, pulled the covers over his head. The knocking continued. In his half-conscious mind, he wondered why his parents weren't getting up. Without thinking, he shouted, *"COME IN."* When he heard a door creak open, he worried immediately he'd made a mistake. Heavy footsteps echoed into the apartment, heading straight for Tony's room. Tony clutched the blankets, clamped his lips shut. The footsteps came directly to the side of his bed. Breath filtered through the covers. Tony flailed as he sat up, but no one was there. Turning on the lamp, he startled to see a yellow envelope lying on the floor.

His payment.

At school the next day, some kids who lived in Matt's neighborhood said the police had been to the Miller house the previous night. His parents had heard some sort of commotion in his room, and when they went in, Matt was gone. His things had been tossed all around, furniture turned over, the window open wide. Worst of all, they said, were the bloody handprints on the windowsill.

Tony couldn't believe it. *Refused* to believe it. Was this his doing? He'd delivered Matt's name to the exterminators. *Exterminators*. He thought back to all the envelopes he had delivered over the past few months. Had they all had a name inside, like Matt's?

There was only one way to be sure: He had to speak with the boss. Before he left school for the day, Tony stopped in the art room and swiped a box cutter.

As he crossed through the gate into the evergreen garden, Tony tried to keep his mind blank, but red handprints marked his imagination.

He paused at the door on the fifth floor, fingered the handle of the blade in his coat pocket. Then he pounded on the door. Again. Again. He smashed the fleshy part of his fist against the metal so many times, his arm ached. When he *did* stop, no sound came from within. As always.

Tony was about to call out, maybe something rude, when there came that familiar shuffling sound. Looking down, he saw a white envelope sticking out from under the door. He picked it up. Pinched it carefully between his thumb and forefinger, as if it were dangerous. A weapon maybe. Anger pulsed behind his eyes and throbbed in his skull. "Where is he? What did you do to him?" Tony kicked the door, leaving a small dent.

When he was almost at the stairwell, a creaking came from behind him. Looking back, he saw the boss's door was open a crack. Impenetrable darkness peered out. The door opened wider.

A shadow in the frame lunged at him.

He bolted.

In the darkened lobby, his shoes slapped against marble, the gold flecks of mica flashing up at him like galaxies swirling in the edges of his vision.

Tony's foot slid as he raced down the subway stairs. When he grabbed at the railing to keep from tumbling onto the empty platform, he accidentally crumpled the envelope in his hand.

"STAND CLEAR OF THE CLOSING DOORS, PLEASE."

As soon as he stepped inside, the train pulled away from the station.

Tony rubbed the envelope on his thigh, smoothing out the newly made creases. The contents were nearly visible through the thin paper. Another scribbled name. He used his nail to pull at the corner. Removed the scrap. Read the name.

Tony nodded. He wanted to feel surprise. Shock, even. But this was the opposite of shock. He'd broken the rules, after all. His own name stared up at him.

Someone coughed.

Tony wasn't alone.

He grabbed at the railing as the train rounded a corner and squealed. The scrap fell from his hand.

Two people sat at the other end of the car. Both wore the same gray jumpsuit. A uniform with a familiar-looking patch on the left breast. A white diamond-shaped emblem, bordered in crimson, with red stitching that read *Ember's Exterminators*. The pair smiled at him.

"Hey, Tony," the woman called out. "Wanna see something scary?" She nudged a large crate by her feet.

The top of the crate came up over the woman's knee. A skittering sound came from within. A clicking. A scraping.

The box juddered forward.

Tony scrambled backward.

He ran to the door at the far side of the car, tried the latch, but it wouldn't move. He leaned against the door as the train shook, speeding up, its momentum throwing him off-balance.

The fluorescents flickered. A bang erupted from the opposite side of the car. A moment later, the lid of the crate was on the floor.

The couple chuckled, and the woman kicked at the box. Something black and leathery peeked up from inside. The lights in the train went out again, but a strobing glow came in from the windows in the tunnel.

Tony caught glimpses of a creature crawling from the

box. It was like someone had glued together pieces from his nightmares. At least six stick-thin legs carried a furry, oblong body. Membranes of slick black skin connected to the front appendages like the wings of a giant bat. As the creature shifted its weight, gaining its equilibrium in the quaking train, Tony heard the click-clack of sharp claws. He reached into his coat pocket for the box-cutter blade, brought it forth, held it like a small sword.

As the creature moved closer, its face became clearer. Its skull was the size of large dog's, but its many midnight-colored eyes were spiderlike, clumped together, reflecting the lights passing outside. The place where a mouth might have been was merely a hole, jammed full of jointed spikes—teeth, or mandibles, or *tools* to shove whatever food it captured into its throat. When the thing had made it past the first set of seats, it paused, tilting its head as if searching. A pair of skin flaps rose up from the sides of its head, ears maybe, and it released a snapping sound that Tony felt in his bones.

"Stop!" he shouted. "Please! Tell the boss . . . Tell him I'm sorry!"

Laughter echoed from the other end of the car as the lights in the tunnel disappeared. The pair in the uniforms, the exterminators, evaporated into a field of black.

As the clicking of claws rushed toward him—*closer, closer*—Tony swung his blade blindly. He imagined what Matt Miller must have experienced the previous night, shortly after Tony had dropped off the envelope at the warehouse near the docks.

The reek of something sweet—too sweet to be *actually* sweet—pierced a spot in his nose, up between his eyes. A moment later, he felt a searing pain slice his chest. Looking down, he saw a crescent-shaped tear, turning his shirt red. The blade slipped from his withering fingers.

"I'm sorry," he tried to whisper as he learned the true purpose of the spikes that jutted from the creature's face.

GILBERT GOES UNDERGROUND

The voice went silent. The cassette hissed quietly though the headphones.

Gilbert's phone chimed—another message from Percy. He pressed the Walkman's STOP button, glad to have an excuse to quit listening to the disconcerting story.

> What's the word?

Gilbert had so much to say, he figured it would be easier to call.

"Yo!" Percy answered with forced cheer.

Gilbert had been so wrapped up in the tale of "Tony" and the exterminators, he'd almost forgotten where he was. The cafeteria was still fairly sleepy. "Hey, Perce."

"How's Ant doing?"

Gilbert related most of what Grandma Rosemary had told him. "It's super weird," he added, "and I'm really scared for

Ant. Like, I never imagined seeing him that way. I don't know what we'd do without him. When I think about what he must have seen . . ." He shuddered. "It's hard to say this, but none of that is even the weirdest—*or scariest*—part." He went into what had happened with the shadowed figure in Ant's room. And finding the leather satchel, the player, the cassettes.

Tales to Keep You Up at Night.

Finally, he mentioned his brother's garbled voicemail from earlier.

Don't listen to the tapes . . .

Percy interrupted. "Please tell me you ignored that request."

Gilbert almost laughed. He loved how well Percy knew him. "Turns out there are *actual* tales on the tapes. I just finished listening to one of them." As he spoke, he noticed a mark on the table. A large black circle, about ten inches across. Like this: **O**. How had he not seen it sooner? "The thing is . . . I think that first story might have been about my brother."

Gilbert shared the tale of the exterminators.

Percy said nothing for a few seconds. "But that sounds like a fantasy story, Gilbert. A *horror* story. Maybe you're looking for meaning where there isn't any?"

Leave it to Percy to bring Gilbert back down to earth.

But how could Percy understand? The strangeness of seeing Ant all messed up in that hospital bed, the shadowed figure, these tapes. Together, it all felt like too much. "It's just . . . the story. The narrator. They were talking, and it was . . . familiar. The character of Tony. We call Ant, *Ant*, but his name's really Antonio."

"I *know* your brother's name, Gilbert."

"In the story, Tony's grandmother is from St. Croix. Our grandma is from St. Thomas."

"And?"

"They're neighboring islands! And . . . *and*, in the story, Tony's friend is named Matt Miller. Ant has a buddy called, get this, *Matthias Mueller*." Percy was quiet now, as if considering. "Weirdest of all, Ant's been coming home late the past few weeks. My parents have been worried about him, but Ant's insisted he had some after-school thing. Just like Tony pretended in the story."

"You're overlooking that giant bat-wolf-spiders do not, in reality, exist. Never have. Facts, kid."

The O was peering up from the table, like an eyeball, glaring into Gilbert's brain. "I mean . . . obviously. It just . . . doesn't feel right."

"How about this," said Percy calmly. "When Ant wakes up, you ask him about his voice message. About the Tony story."

"He told me not to listen."

"The least of your worries."

"But how did Ant know I'd find the tapes at all? After everything, in my head, I'm like, *What's real? What's not?*"

Percy sighed. "You're just stressed."

"What if Ant doesn't wake up? What then?"

"He's where he needs to be. He's safe. Your grandma is there. Want me to meet you too?"

Gilbert wished he could hug them.

"Thanks, but it's really far, and we've—"

The phone chimed again, this time with a notification from Grandma Rosemary.

It read: *Come back now!*

Gilbert found her standing in the noisy hallway upstairs, bouncing on her toes.

"Oh, Gilbert," she cried, and then squeezed him.

"What's wrong now?" he managed to ask through new panic.

"He was having trouble breathing. And then *this* happened." She gestured through the doorway. Ant's room was filled with medical staff. Alarms were blaring. People were shouting.

A woman approached from the nursing station. "The waiting room is just down the hall." As she led the way, Gilbert caught bits of what the emergency staff were saying. "More tests . . . Possible poisoning . . ."

"My brother was *poisoned*?" he asked.

"I don't have that information, honey." The waiting room was filled with navy blue armchairs and gray couches. A wide window overlooked the river. The sky was nearly drained of daylight, the brightest stars beginning to peek through a pinkish scrim of light pollution. "I'll let you know more when I can."

The door closed, blocking out the wild sounds of the unit. Gilbert grabbed his grandmother's hand, forced her to sit beside him on one of the stiff couches.

It felt like they'd wandered into another dimension.

With a gasp, Grandma Rosemary jolted. "I've got to phone your parents!"

To distract himself, Gilbert grabbed the library book from the satchel. The epigraph on the first page read: *May these plants find you when you need them most, same as this book.* This was followed by countless photographs of vegetation, flowers, and herbs; however, the names and descriptions were like something from fantasy stories. One caught his eye. *Goblin's Tongue, or Gremlin's Tongue, can be found on the fifth island from the water-gate in the Frozen-Summer Sea. Place the petals behind your bottom front teeth, and you will know the language of the beasts who live there.* The book wasn't what he'd expected it to be, and he wondered if Percy might tease him for thinking it was anything but fiction. Percy could be a snob about botany. Once, when they were making tea mixes from their community garden plot, Gilbert added a bunch of monkshood instead of mugwort, and Percy freaked, asking if he was trying to poison them both. Maybe this wasn't snobbery; maybe it was just smarts.

As he flipped through more pages, Grandma Rosemary made more calls.

Gilbert kept drifting back to the story about the exterminators—how it mirrored a version of Ant's life, provided a kind of absurd explanation for what was going on today. In the tale, Tony had listened to a bunch of tapes his friend Matt had given him. In real life, Ant had told Gilbert to *not* listen to the tapes.

So then: Was the connection hidden on the rest of the tapes?

Gilbert messaged Percy to apologize for hanging up; however, what he wanted to do was set those headphones over his ears again, see what else the narrator had to say. The ending of Tony's tale felt abrupt, but then, sometimes scary stories were like that. Kept you wondering. *Worrying.* Gilbert almost dared to pull out the Walkman again, but he couldn't risk Grandma Rosemary taking it away. Who knew what voicemails Ant had left *her*?

To his relief, Grandma Rosemary told him to leave. "Your parents can't make it back to the city till tomorrow, so for tonight, you'll stay at my house. Okay?"

"With Auntie Sheila?" Gilbert groaned, knowing he sounded like a snot, but he couldn't help it. They'd never gotten along. To Gilbert's credit, Auntie Sheila didn't get along with *anyone*. Not even Grandma Rosemary.

"Yes." Grandma Rosemary's tone was a caution. "She's got

oxtail simmering for you. And johnnycakes. And she's already made up the bed on the pull-out couch."

The one with the bar that can break a spine? "I was thinking I might stay at a friend's house instead."

Flustered, Grandma Rosemary rummaged through her purse. "No, Gilbert, I think it's best we don't disrupt another family's evening. Sheila's expecting you. Please don't argue." She winced as she removed her wallet. "I don't have cash for you to take a taxi."

"The train is fine."

"But it's getting dark."

"Mom and Dad let me do it all the time." What he didn't say was: *On the train, I can listen to the tapes.*

"When you're with your brother, they do." Imagining Ant riding the subway alone jabbed a needle into Gilbert's chest. "All right," she said with a sigh. "If you promise to call me as *soon* as you get there. And if you don't talk to strangers. And—"

"I'm not a baby."

She grabbed at his hands, looked into his eyes. "What worries me is that you're not a grown-up either."

Ouch.

On the street, the wind tried to bite him again, but Gilbert grabbed his coat around his middle. Rush hour was in full swing, and the sidewalks were crowded. He held tight to the leather satchel, feeling the cassettes, the player, and the library book bounce against his side as he walked briskly to the station.

Gilbert skidded into a seat near the door. There was that familiar announcement, "*STAND CLEAR OF THE CLOSING DOORS, PLEASE.*" The *BING-BONG* chimes rang, then the train jerked into the tunnel. Grasping the Walkman, he started the next tale.

THE SEASHELL

Emma had been drifting in and out of sleep when the car jolted to a stop.

The safety belt grabbed at her shoulder, and she opened her eyes, gasping. Her first instinct had been to lash out at her brother beside her. Glenn had poked and prodded her the whole ride down from the college, where their father had been the guest lecturer at the library that morning.

"What was that for?!" he yelped when she smacked his arm.

Exasperated, Mom turned around in the passenger seat. "Are we going to have to leave you two in the car?"

More awake now, Emma realized that Dad had not yet pulled back into the rental lot in the city. Instead, they'd parked in a weird kind of . . .

Nether-space?

Daylight was dim. She couldn't guess the time. A dense mist, masking the world outside the windows, made her wonder if a dream had followed her into the waking world.

"Where are we?"

Dad unbuckled his seat belt. "The fog got so bad on the highway, driving didn't feel safe. We pulled off until it clears up."

Emma looked again. This was no dream, only a parking lot.

"What if it *doesn't* clear up?" Glenn asked.

"Then I guess we'll just have to stay in this sleepy little town forever," Dad answered.

From the rearview mirror, Emma noticed a glint in his eyes. Sometimes, her father's teasing was just as bad as Glenn's.

Mom opened her door. "There must be a cute little clam shack or something open around here."

From outside, there came a monstrous roar. Emma cringed and let out a soft squeal.

Glenn burst out laughing. "What's *wrong* with you?"

Emma's mind was still teetering on the edge of sleep, so she'd misheard the rolling of ocean waves as something scary. But now the sound was clear. Constant. *Whooshhhh*. Her face flushed. She spat back, "Nothing! What's wrong with *you*?"

Stepping onto cracked asphalt, she felt a damp chill. She zipped up her jacket. During October in the Northeast, the temperature often turned like a weathervane in a storm. Salt infused the air, tickled Emma's nose. In the distance, she could barely make out the silhouettes of hunched buildings. Except for their little rental, the beach lot was empty.

Emma's family had left home early the previous day, had spent the night at a bed and breakfast a couple miles from the college where her father was to speak. The trip was supposed to have been a brief getaway, not only for their father's academic visit, but for the rest of them to peep the changing foliage up north.

"There are people in the water," Glenn shouted. He'd walked onto the sand about twenty yards from the boardwalk.

People? What people? Emma thought. *The water must be almost freezing.* With this fog, even surfers in wetsuits might struggle to navigate the rocky coast. Glenn loved getting a rise out of her. "Stop trying to freak us out," she called to him.

"I swear! Beyond the breakers. They're . . . staring at us."

Staring?

Mom focused her camera past the shoreline and zoomed in. "He's right," she whispered. She pressed the shutter button.

Dad sidled stiffly beside her, holding his hand over his brow. "Who are they?"

Emma hated being left out of the joke. She took off after Glenn, finding him where the foam rolled a thin line across wet sand. She saw them finally—floating far beyond where the waves churned. Her chest tightened.

"*Mermaids*," Glenn whispered, still teasing.

"No such thing," she said to her brother, but it was more as if she needed to convince herself.

"I think they're seals." Dad had crept up behind her. "As curious about us as we are about them." Then he chuckled. "Stay away, kids. Around here, great whites love to snatch them up for lunch."

"We'd need to be in the water to worry about that," Glenn said, unsurely.

"I see you've never heard of land sharks."

"Carl, leave them alone!" Mom was still by the boardwalk.

"Fathers are meant to warn their families of such dangers, no?" Emma could hear the smirk in his voice.

"Know what else fathers are supposed to do?" Mom answered. "Find food when mothers are hungry."

"Thanks for the warning, Dad." Emma sniffed, trying to sound annoyed. She actually thought her parents were pretty funny, but she couldn't let them know. They'd try to be funny all the time.

Seals. Maybe later, she'd research and then share what she found with her science teacher, Mrs. Chung.

Emma *loved* extra credit.

Ahead, through the mist, large letters appeared. FUN-O-RAMA. An arcade? Glenn got there first. "'Closed for the Season,'" he read, pointing at a sign beside the shuttered steel rolltop gate.

"That stinks," said Emma, trying at the same time to ignore the actual stink of low tide. "Don't they know people want to have fun even *after* summer ends?"

At the edge of the boardwalk, Glenn crouched, slipped down, then scrambled deftly across the boulders.

"Where are you going?" Emma shouted.

"To find cool stuff in the tidal pools!"

She wanted to tell him to come back, but she was afraid he'd make fun of her again. She lowered herself onto a flat rock speckled with barnacles, crusty seaweed, reddish stains from rust, minerals, algae. That low-tide stink was all-powerful. Holding her breath, Emma crossed large gaps between the stones. Here were the tidal pools—filled with creamy foam and congregations of snails tucked neatly inside their spiral shells. Emma dipped her fingers in the water. *Scary* cold.

Those seals beyond the surf must have some super-thick layer of fat to keep themselves warm.

"Careful, you two!" Mom sounded far away.

Glenn was still at least twenty feet out, on one of the lower rocks, peering into the crevice below.

Emma noticed an interesting object by the pool next to his feet. Something black. Shiny. Covered with spines sharp enough to pierce straight through the soles of sneakers. "Be careful, Glenn."

When Glenn saw the thing in the pool, he scooped it up. "Whoa—"

"What *is* that?" An urchin, she imagined. She thought of poison and barbs and hospital rooms.

"A seashell." He held the object up for her to see. Its surface glinted, even in the muted light.

Not an urchin. Some mollusk, maybe. It was huge! About a foot across. The black spikes rising from the coil of its body looked dangerous and beautiful. "I've never seen one like that," she heard herself say. But hadn't she? In a book in Mrs. Chung's classroom? Yes, a Venus's-comb. But those had been white. Alabaster. This one looked like it had been dipped in hot tar. "Is anything inside?"

Glenn shook the shell, then gazed into its crevice. "Looks empty." He held it to his ear.

Instantly, his face went blank.

Something splashed in the nearby pool, but Glenn didn't notice. Nervous, Emma called, "Come back?"

But it was like he couldn't, or wouldn't, hear her.

Something twined out of the tidal pool near his foot. A tentacle? Cephalopods sometimes left the ocean, didn't they? Octopuses. Squids. Creatures with eyes like a goat's and suckers all up and down their arms. Was the pool by Glenn's feet deeper than it looked? "Glenn?" Her voice was wobbly.

With the spiky shell at his ear, his expression was frozen, as if in bafflement . . . or maybe fright.

Barking echoed out on the water. All at once, the seals dipped below the surface. "Glenn." Emma's voice trembled. "I think you should come up here, like, *now*."

The squirming shape in the pool jerked around his ankle. Glenn yelped and leaped away, his sneakers slipping on the slick stone. The tentacle slid quickly back into the pool with barely a splash. Gripping the shell to his chest, Glenn scurried toward Emma's flat stone by the boardwalk. "Something grabbed me!" He tucked the shell under his other arm. Its shiny black spikes pressed into his jacket.

"I saw." Emma couldn't unglue her gaze from the object cradled in the crook of his elbow. "It was only seaweed," she fibbed. She wasn't sure why. "You got a little tangled up."

"Seaweed?" Glenn whispered. Mist now obscured the pool. "It felt like—"

"Just a bit of seaweed," Emma insisted.

Her skin tingled. *Was it the chill? Or was it something else?* She felt an odd desire to push him down, snatch the seashell. Hold it up to her own ear.

"What are you up to down there?" Mom's voice was right behind them. Dad crouched, presented helping hands, and pulled them up off the rock.

"I found a seashell!" Glenn exclaimed, as if he had no memory of the tidal pool.

"And what a seashell it is," said Mom. "Let me take a picture."

"Can we bring it home?" Emma asked.

"It's *my* shell," Glenn answered with a side glance.

Emma gave him one right back.

In the parking lot, Glenn placed the shell in the car's trunk.

Up the road, a hazy light illuminated the door of a restaurant called the Blue Lobster. "Who's hungry?" asked Mom.

After the parents paid the bill, the family returned to their car. By then, the fog had blown away. Sparkling starlight blanketed the indigo sky, interrupted only by the black horizon.

On the walk, Dad and Mom conversed quietly while Emma and Glenn whispered to themselves. "When you held that shell to your ear, it looked like you got hypnotized," she said.

"Hypnotized?" Glenn's skin turned a shade of gray. "I don't remember."

Emma considered him. "Yes, you do," she pushed. Not to be annoying, but because she was truly intrigued.

He kicked at a piece of gravel. Glenn was usually a confident kid. But now ... "I heard a voice, whispering inside it."

That was not what Emma had expected. "What did it say?"

"It sounded like ... *Put me down.*"

She smirked. "You *heard* that?"

"And then ... I think ... There was screaming."

Her eyebrow popped up in surprise. "*Screaming?*" she echoed, wanting to laugh. But Glenn's eyes were glazed over, his mind far away. "Inside the seashell?" He nodded. She remembered the rubbery appendage and how it had tried to loop his ankle. "Why didn't you drop it?"

His empty gaze met her eyes, then he shrugged.

"Lovely night," Mom interrupted, whipping out her camera again. She adjusted the settings for a long exposure of the coast.

"Mm." Dad clicked the key fob, and the lights blinked on as the sedan's doors unlocked. That's when they saw one of the taillights was cracked. Scratches marked the paint around the trunk, and the license plate was bent. "Who would do this?" Dad asked.

Emma couldn't help glancing toward the ocean.

As their parents discussed rental insurance, she and Glenn approached the trunk. Clearly, someone, or something, had wanted to get at the black seashell. Glenn felt for the latch, and the trunk popped open. The shell sat inside. Safe and sound.

Emma felt her hands rise, as if to grasp for it, but Glenn blocked her. She tried to shake him off, but he planted his feet. She was about to shout when he whispered harshly, "That voice I heard inside the shell—" He grabbed her shoulders and forced her to face him. His eyes were deep pools. "The voice . . . ," he choked out. "It was *yours*."

Emma felt herself freeze up.

But only for a moment.

He was joking, obviously. "Jerk," she said, then reached up and slammed the trunk closed again. Her thumb came away slick with something that felt like mucus. She shuddered and wiped it on her jeans.

Mom took the wheel this time. "Hopefully, by now, city traffic will have died down."

Dad agreed. "The car's due back in about two hours."

Mom pressed her foot on the gas and said, "Vroom, vroom, babies."

Dad chuckled, but Emma was distracted. She looked to her brother. If he'd only been teasing, why did he look worried?

At home, Emma mustered the energy to search the internet for seashells with large spikes. The most intriguing result was a type of sea snail called a murex that produced a purple-blue secretion some people used as dye. But none were black or shiny. None were as beautiful as the one that had appeared on those rocks, like a gift from the sea.

In the night, Emma shuddered out of sleep. When she sat up, she heard Mom and Dad and Glenn through the wall. Her brother sounded upset. Were those sobs or was he choking? She crept to the cracked door.

". . . only a nightmare, honey . . ."

". . . Where's Emma . . . ?"

". . . asleep, in her room . . ."

Then came a shout of anger. Horror. "Get it away from me! I don't want it in my bedroom!"

Quick footsteps moved into the hallway. Dad carried the seashell delicately down the corridor.

Mom was making soothing sounds, like lullabies, as if Glenn had suddenly turned into a baby. He'd had some kind of bad dream. About the seashell? Bad enough to make him behave like this? Emma couldn't remember the last time she'd had a nightmare like that. Dad went back to his own bedroom, but Mom stayed with Glenn. Lamplight sliced at the floor.

When things grew quiet again, Emma peered around the corner. Mom had passed out beside Glenn. At the apartment's front door, she turned the knob, careful that it didn't squeak.

The mass of black caught her eye. Her father had left the seashell on the doormat like a piece of trash. Emma's eyes stung. How dare he? How dare any of them?

The seashell. Was not. *Trash*.

She scooped it up. Back in her bedroom, Emma sat cross-legged on her mattress, the seashell before her. She was tempted to hold it to her ear, as Glenn had done at the beach. But a nagging thought told her not to. Instead, she grabbed her book bag off the back of her desk chair, then slipped the seashell inside.

"Your brother's not feeling well," Mom said later, as Emma emerged into the kitchen for breakfast. She was showered, dressed, and ready, her backpack dangling from her shoulder. If Mom had looked closely, she would have noticed the strange bulge inside. "He's staying home today."

Emma flinched. "Is he all right?"

"I think he just needs some rest. It was a busy weekend."

Emma sighed. It had been busy for her too, but you didn't see her trying to get out of going to school. In fact, Emma couldn't wait to reach homeroom. To show Mrs. Chung what she'd found. "I should head out," she said. "Tell Glenn I hope he feels better."

The day was shiny and blue, a far cry from the weekend weather. The October breeze whisked down the city streets, putting a weightlessness in Emma's step. There was also the pull of the straps from her book bag against her shoulders. The spikes from the seashell pressed into her spine. Still, she was certain Mrs. Chung would congratulate her on such a magnificent find.

By the time she reached the school, cool sweat made her shirt cling. In the third-floor bathroom, she slipped the bag off her shoulders and set it in the sink. Looking in the mirror, she gasped. The bottom of her jacket was sopping wet—not with sweat, but with some purplish liquid. Musty, salty, strange. Her book bag was also soaked, black spikes peeking out from between the edges of the open zipper.

A loud thump sounded from one of the closed toilet stalls.

Emma froze. "Hello? Who's in here?"

Holding the seashell before herself, she stepped toward the stall.

WHAM.

Something hit against the closed door so hard, its hinges shook. Emma flinched back against the wall.

WHAM.

This time, the door swung outward, shivering with the force. Emma yelped. A shape swung up from the toilet bowl. Water splashed to the floor, rushed across the tile.

She dashed for the exit. In the mirror above the sink, she caught sight of a dark form quivering out of the stall.

Emma grabbed the door handle and scrambled into the hallway, then watched the door close softly behind her. Her breath was rough. Her temples throbbed, and her mind went nearly blank with panic.

The hall was filled with a kind of mist. Grasping the seashell to her chest, she noticed now that her hands had turned that purplish color, as if dipped in dye.

Dark water poured out from the space under the door, surrounding the soles of her shoes. A meaty, slapping sound came from inside. The mist swirled thickly, and a stench of low tide made Emma dizzy.

"Hello?" she called out again. There was silence. And a kind of ... hissing ...

The seashell's spikes niggled at her ribs. It felt heavy

now. Instinct told her to toss it away, let it shatter. Her brain shouted, *STOP. NO. KEEP IT CLOSE.*

The bathroom door opened, revealing a tall shape, enshrouded by mist.

Emma teetered. The seashell slipped, skittered across the floor. She landed, palms down, leaving dark handprints on damp wooden planks. Water soaked her knees. She sat, scuttled backward.

Fog swooped all around. Beyond, neon lights filtered through the atmosphere, crimson letters reading FUN-O-RAMA. That hissing sound was distinct now—the ocean, just down a familiar slope of boulders.

Emma shivered, reached for the seashell, pulled it close.

Appendages smacked against the boardwalk. The shape was upon her. From the misty shroud, tentacles emerged. They wrapped around her shoulders, her chest, and then clenched. Sharp bites stung where suckers latched.

Then she was up, her feet kicking wildly. Emma tried to catch her breath. But the tentacles squeezed tighter. She managed to hold on to the slick spikes of the seashell, but now those hurt too. Her eyeballs swelled with pressure. Still, she stared, closer now, determined to comprehend the thing that had emerged from the girls' room. Through a flurry of fear, she discerned a wide head, a pair of dark impressions where the animal's eyes might be.

She forced out the words: "Put ... me ... down ..."

Memory crashed like a wave—what her brother had told her yesterday, about holding the seashell to his ear. She'd just echoed him. But what had he claimed came next?

A glint in the thing's dark eyes shifted from her face and toward the onyx seashell in her clenched hands. A grumbling, glottal sound rose up inside her brain, and it took her a moment to understand that it was a voice. Long. Drawn out. Like the last line of a low dirge. It said:

MINE.

"Put . . . me . . . down!"

Again, the thing spoke:

MIIIIINE.

Its arms squeezed. She could barely take a breath.

"Want this?" Emma wheezed. She lifted the shell toward the thing's face, or what she imagined was a face. The mist swirled upon it like a veil, as if Mother Nature knew that looking directly upon it might do bad things to Emma's mind. "Take . . . it . . ." The words almost hurt to speak. Not because her lungs were squeezed nearly flat. But because, despite everything, she knew the shell was *hers*.

Another tentacle emerged from inside the mist, ruby red, pulsating. For a moment, Emma could see the rest of this thing's body. It was *all tentacle*—a mass of flesh and suckers and slime, seaweed and ratted rope and pieces of coral and bone and *shipwrecks*, and other treasures it had captured from deep water. The end of this new tentacle curled around the shell. The creature lifted it away from Emma's grip, and suddenly, she felt free.

As if a spell had been broken.

She let out a sob of relief. "Take it," she managed to tell the creature. "Let me go."

The creature considered the spiky black object for a long moment—the object it had traveled so far to claim. Its grip loosened.

Air flushed into Emma's lungs. Once the creature had its treasure back, it would leave her alone. The mist would disappear. The hallway would return. As would her schoolmates. And Mrs. Chung. And Glenn, sick in bed at home, where Emma wished to be.

The creature from the pool tossed the seashell away. It clattered across the blurry boardwalk.

The squeeze at Emma's shoulders and chest tightened again, the suckers biting her skin harder. She arched her spine, tried to wriggle away, but there was a pinch, and suddenly, she couldn't move at all. The creature's black eyes refocused. That gleam, that glimmer, that glint—maybe a reflection of the arcade's crimson signage, or maybe a fire that glowed within—grew brighter, and the dark voice rumbled again through Emma's skull.

MIIIIIINNNNNNNE.

It no longer wanted the shell . . .

They were moving together now, shifting upon the wooden planks.

The creature reached the pool where Emma had first spotted the mass of black spikes—the treasure she'd believed would impress her teacher.

As the creature lowered itself into the pool, dragging Emma along with it, she finally understood.

She was the treasure now.

She was worth *everything in the world*.

The water slipped up over her shoulders, then her neck, her chin, her lips, nose, eyes. It enveloped the crown of her skull, pearlescent bubbles gleaming. Salt stung her throat, her stomach, her lungs.

But this didn't feel bad. It felt . . . *new*.

Above, Emma heard turning waves, an endless spiraling rhythm. From far away, there came the frenzied barking of those seals, her court.

Pink sparks rose up from purple darkness.

And she was glad.

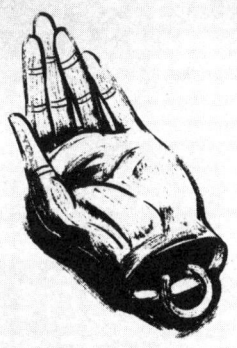

GIFTS FROM UNDER THE BED

Quiana Thompson's attic bedroom was the smallest in the house. Her father had built it when her stepmother had become pregnant and they all realized they'd need more space for a new kid. Its slanted walls were the insides of the roof, covered with insulation and drywall. If you weren't wearing thick socks in winter, the plank floors were bone-chilling. With one slim window, the place was a little gloomy, but Quiana's dad had strung up pink Christmas lights in a zigzag pattern across the purple ceiling. Over her bed, she'd taped posters of her favorite singers: Whitney Houston, Janet Jackson, Madonna. Of everything in her room, her bed was her favorite—wide and fluffy, with pillows as soft as clouds. For a cover, there was the violet patchwork quilt her mother had made when she'd been sick and couldn't get up out of her *own* bed anymore. In the drawer in the nightstand was

Quiana's journal. If you were to inspect the pages, you'd find entries about her mother's passing, about her father meeting Jody, their wedding, Jody's pregnancy, and finally the birth of her brother, Dax. Once, jotting down her thoughts helped Quiana feel less anxious about thinking them in the first place. It is the journal I would ask you to examine, for within these pages are clues to Quiana's fate—clues that her family, and the authorities, had once dismissed as a ten-year-old's fantastical imaginings. Go on. Open the drawer. Take it out. Flip to the back, where the last five entries are buried. Begin your reading at the first of them, on that final Monday. Quiana won't mind. She won't even know. As you may have already guessed, the girl no longer lives here.

Monday—The Velvet Box

I found a present on my pillow this morning, right next to my head, wrapped in plain brown paper and tied with black string that looped through a notecard with the word LISTEN written in red pencil. I thought maybe Dad snuck into my room in the night to surprise me. But downstairs, when I showed him, he looked at me like I was making things up again.

Even when I opened the wrapping in front of him, he didn't believe me. He said that telling stories isn't nice. I yelled that I wasn't telling stories, and he told me to shush but I wouldn't shush because someone left a present on my pillow. I asked Jody if she was the one who did it but she was busy feeding Dax which makes me think she didn't do it either. Inside the wrapping was a fuzzy black box. Velvet I think. The lid has hinges. It fits in the palm of my hand.

In my room when I flipped it open I heard someone whispering but I couldn't understand what they were saying. The box was empty. No small speakers like in spy movies. Even when I held it close to my ear, I couldn't make out the whispering. It's like this <u>shuh-shuh-shuh-shuh</u>. I tried to make Dad listen but he shook his head and looked at me like I was trying to be annoying. He should know by now that if I want to be annoying I have many other ways.

Tonight I was lying in bed with the velvet box. The whispering makes me see things in my mind. Weird swirling shadows. A couple times I noticed faces looking at me from behind my eyelids. Then I heard noises under my bed. A clicking came every few seconds. It made me think of secret codes. I wondered if it was a mouse like the one Dad caught last year. I definitely didn't want that so I was slightly freaked out. I peeked over the edge of my mattress but it was dark and I couldn't see anything. When I closed the lid, the clicking stopped.

Tuesday—The Silver Lilac
There was another present on my bed this morning but not on my pillow. This one was on my mother's quilt close to

my shoulder. A flower like something I didn't know existed. I think it's a lilac but the petals are silver. They shine pink underneath the lights Dad hung on my ceiling. The flower wasn't wrapped in paper. But there was another black thread tied around the stem just like on the velvet box. Also, there was a notecard. Red pencil said BREATHE.

And since that's what you're supposed to do around flowers I held the lilac to my nose and took a big whiff. The scent was so sweet, it made me feel almost dizzy.

<u>Dizzy</u> isn't the exact right word. I felt like I was floating. Like my bedroom was far away. I checked my feet though and I was still on the floor.

Downstairs, Dad was getting ready for work again. I showed him the flower and the note. He frowned like I was trying to make him late. That made me mad. Someone is leaving me gifts in the night I told him. And he said that there were better ways to ask for attention. My face got so hot it could have burned the house down. I don't want attention I yelled. Dad and Jody think I'm jealous of Dax. But I'm not. I swear! And if I was why would I pretend to give myself weird gifts with notes like LISTEN and BREATHE? It's not something a kid like me would do. I made Jody smell the silver lilac and she said mmm pretty. She didn't look dizzy or like she might start floating. This made me wonder. Dad hadn't heard the velvet box whispering. Jody couldn't smell what I'd smelled. Were these things in my head? Or did it mean that the two presents were meant <u>only</u> for me?

The weirdest part happened at bedtime. Again. I'd turned out my lights and was listening to the <u>shuh-shuh-shuh</u> from the velvet box when I caught a whiff of the silver lilac on my nightstand. For the first time, I thought I could make out words in the whispers. I smelled the flower as hard as I could and then inside the floating feeling I heard my name coming from the box. A soft voice repeated <u>Quiana, Quiana, Quiana.</u> Over and over. An echo. Behind my eyelids, the faces became clearer. They were smiling. I tried talking to the box. I asked what it wanted. But it wouldn't say anything other than my name.

<u>Wednesday—The Crystal Orb</u>

Would you be surprised to learn that this morning there was another present? It wasn't on my bed at all but sitting on the table with my lamp, a few inches away from my pillow. This one was a polished sphere made from some pink stone on a dark wooden stand. And tied around the base, another string with another note. This one said SEE.

When I showed it to Dad at breakfast he got really mad. Maybe it was because I was sort of tearing up and shivery from excitement and he doesn't like seeing me that way. For the first time I really really believed that Dad <u>isn't</u> the one who's leaving these things for me. He even threatened to take the crystal orb away if I didn't stop pretending and making a big deal out of everything. He said I should pay more attention to Dax and help out around the house and be a team player. And then he asked if this was because they'd moved my room up to the attic when the baby was born so Dax could have the bigger bedroom right next to theirs. And I said NO and then I really started crying even though I didn't want to. Jody stepped in and stopped Dad from taking my orb. She gave him a hug and sent him out to his car and then came and kissed my forehead which I only put up with because she'd just been so kind. Then she told me to get ready for school, so I did.

    What I didn't tell her was that I packed up my three gifts in a sturdy box from the pantry and brought them with me on the bus. At school I showed the box the flower and the orb to Doris and Michaela and without telling them how the presents showed up I asked what they thought. Doris and Michaela didn't hear the whispering. They weren't impressed by the lilac's scent but they agreed it was a beautiful treasure and I was lucky to find it and the rest of them too.

    I skipped gym class and hid in the equipment closet with my gifts instead. If the velvet box whispered my name after I sniffed the floaty flower, I figured the orb must do something too. Its note said SEE. So I sat on the floor and stared into the polished crystal. And before I knew it figures were dancing around inside. Not only in the orb. I saw them inside my head too. They were waving at me. I kind of wish I could dance with them because it looks like they're having lots of fun. Afterward I didn't bother asking Doris and Michaela if they noticed anything weird about the orb because I knew they wouldn't. And if I told them about the dancing I knew they'd just get jealous and tell me I was lying again. I've only lied to them like four times so I don't know why they think I'm that type of person.

Thursday—The Berry Bracelet
Today's gift was on the floor beside the bed. I almost stepped on it barefoot. Lucky I didn't cut myself. This one is a bracelet made of twisted copper-colored wire with an opening at the back like the cuff my mom sometimes wore. Costume jewelry. At the front three large red stones are tangled up as if magic holds them in place. The notecard attached to the black string said TASTE. So I sat on my bed, slipped the cuff onto my wrist, and then touched the tip of my tongue to one of the stones. It made me feel weird in a way that's hard to explain. The inside of my mouth went smooth. There wasn't really a flavor except maybe like when you bite your cheek and get a hint of blood. I put the other gifts in the center of my mattress and then tested them in order. I opened the velvet box and inhaled the lilac's scent and stared into the pink orb. There were dancing figures

and I heard the voice whisper my name. I asked what they wanted, and they seemed to actually <u>finally</u> hear me. The voice said <u>Come with us.</u> Which I thought was kind of scary at first but then the people in the orb waved and I heard them laughing and playing happy music. I had a feeling they wouldn't accuse me of telling stories and making things up and lying and wanting attention. Where they are there won't be babies crying in the middle of the night and they won't stick me in an attic bedroom like a fairy-tale princess that broke some dumb rule made by some dumb king. Where are you? I asked them. The voice from the velvet box whispered <u>Underneath.</u> And I said Underneath what? And it answered <u>Underneath your bed.</u>

That gave me chills. I closed the box. I took off the bracelet and went down to the bathroom to brush that smooth metallic feeling out of my mouth.

Is it possible that Dad's right and all of this is in my head? I want to ask him again and maybe tell him more about the other gifts and what they can do. But if he took them away, I think I'd break into pieces. No one else in the world has what I have. I'm sure of it.

<u>Come with us.</u> That's what the voice said. They want me. They need me.

If I go and then come back maybe I could bring Doris and Michaela with me next time to prove everything to everyone. The thing is I don't know how to get there.

Friday—The Golden Hand

There was another gift today but I didn't notice until I got home from school. Coming into my bedroom I saw something shining just underneath my bed frame. A gold sculpture of a hand. It was smaller than a doll's hand but bigger than one of the pieces you use to move around a Monopoly board. Its fingers were pressed together making its middle look like a cup. There was a loop at the wrist, and it made me wonder if it was supposed to be a charm for a charm bracelet. The black thread was tied there. This card said HOLD.

When I pressed it into my palm I saw something in the gap between my mattress and the floor. An extra space that hadn't been there before, with a set of steps leading down, down, down. The sight made my brain wobble. What I saw was impossible. There's no room in my house where this staircase should fit.

I remembered the other gifts. And what I'd learned from them over the past few days. The voice saying <u>Come with us...</u> And I got nervous because here was a way to do it. I dropped the golden hand on my mattress and in a blink the staircase under my bed disappeared. I reached out and tapped the floor just to make sure and I remembered the other night when I'd heard that clicking. I squeezed the golden hand again and the staircase came back. I wanted to call for Jody to make her see what I was seeing. But if she told Dad and he took the hand away from me, my last chance to figure out what was going on would disappear.

Instead, I gathered the other gifts together. I opened the velvet box, sniffed the silver lilac, peered into the crystal orb, and then licked the red stones on the copper cuff. Then holding the hand I stared under the bed. A pinkish glow appeared far below where it looked like the staircase might end. Are you there? I asked. And the voice answered me. <u>We are here. Are you ready?</u> I didn't know what to say because I didn't feel ready. At all. But then something other than dancing shadows came into shape inside the orb. It was a face. This one was clear. When I saw it I almost burst out crying.

My mother's eyes were peering up at me. Pleading. I've never told anyone this before but since she died my one wish has been to see her again. To hold her hand and smell her sweet shampoo and listen to stories about when she was a little girl like me and eat the strawberries she'd cut up for us whenever I got home from school. She knew strawberries were my favorite but I don't think she knew they were my favorite because they were her favorite too.

A new voice came from the velvet box. Loud and clear. It was my mother's voice. She said, <u>I'm waiting, Quiana. Hurry.</u>

I went to my wardrobe and took out my overnight bag. I stuffed it with some socks and underwear and a few pairs of pants and shirts and sweaters in case it's cold down there. I grabbed my toiletry bag from the bathroom downstairs and shoved in my toothbrush and one of those small tubes of toothpaste for traveling. In the pantry I took a box of granola bars and some cans of soup and a can opener and some matches. (You never know when you might need matches.) I put everything into the bag along with the gifts from this week.

All of them except the golden hand, which I stuck in my pocket.

I don't think it's fair to head off down the staircase without telling my family. But I also know that if I say what I'm actually doing they'll scoff like always and say Oh, Quiana, you silly thing.

I decided to tell them something different.

Jody was in the den sitting at her work desk stringing beads through twine to sell at craft fairs every weekend. Dax slept in his vibrating baby chair on the floor beside her. I said Jody I'm going away for a while. She looked up at me and smiled like she wanted to laugh. But I didn't smile back. I wanted her to know I was serious. Where are you headed? she asked me. I said Some friends invited me to come for a visit. Just thought you should know. She had this look like she didn't believe me. Then she answered I hope you have a good time. And: Hopefully you'll be home for dinner when your dad gets back from the office. We'll see I said. Then

I kissed Dax on his baby-sweet forehead and I came back upstairs to write all this down.

I'm leaving this journal on my bed in case anyone needs to know what happened to me. In case I don't come back.

I'm clutching the gold hand now. I've looped the strap of my bag over my shoulder. I'm scared but also excited. The pink light at the bottom of the stairs is pulsing slightly like a breath and a heartbeat and a clock.

I hear Mom's voice muffled coming from the box in my bag. <u>Hurry...</u> I see the fog in my brain and the shadow figures dancing and her wet eyes staring up at me. <u>Hurry, Quiana...</u>

So that's what I'm going to do.

THE FIFTH CEMETERY

At seventeen, Audrina's older sister, Cat, got her driver's license.

Cat's best friend, Helen, suggested a day trip to a college town about an hour from their own village, to visit the five historic cemeteries that people said were haunted. According to legend, if you visited all five before sunset, ghosts would appear. Audrina had always thought Helen was odd. Helen claimed to be an *empath* and a *psychic medium* and that she could *hear spirits whispering after dark*. However, this didn't stop Audrina from asking if she and Damian, her friend from next door, could come with them. Of course, Cat didn't want two twelve-year-olds tagging along, but when Audrina complained, their mother made Cat agree.

Despite what Helen said, Audrina didn't believe in the legend of the cemeteries. She merely wanted to go on the drive, get away from their cul-de-sac for a little while.

The Saturday morning was clear, and the air was crisp

and still. The girls and Damian packed Mom's '84 Accord—five years young and full of pep—with snacks and bottles of water for the drive. "Use this to get there and back," Mom said, handing over the small black box that their father had brought home from work earlier that summer. It looked like a speed-trap detector, but Audrina understood that it was something else—an electronic map device that would speak directions aloud as you drove, using a voice that sounded like a robot.

In half a mile, turn right onto Hardscrabble Road.

Her father had tried it out a few times to find their way to the lake in the hills and also the bike trails by the creek. He'd called it a *prototype*—something brand-new that wasn't available to the general public. He worked for a company called November Corp., and they were constantly giving him access to all sorts of cool gadgets. This one used a new kind of technology called *GPS*, which stood for *Global Positioning System*. Supposedly satellites were involved, which Audrina thought was pretty rad.

When they were ready to go, Cat sat behind the wheel. Helen took shotgun. Audrina and Damian were in the back. Helen had made a mixtape for the occasion. Siouxsie and the Banshees, and Echo and the Bunnymen, and the Cure. Every time Helen instructed them about a song or a band, Audrina and Damian would glance at each other and roll their eyes and giggle quietly. They were twelve, not ignorant.

Damian was new to their neighborhood. *New-ish*. His family had moved in a little over a year prior. Only recently did Audrina wonder if she might have a crush on him. The way he looked at her, with solid eye contact and a wide-open expression, filled with curiosity, made her think he felt the same way. But Mom had told her she wasn't allowed to have a boyfriend until at least high school. An eternity away.

The GPS device took them along back roads, the robot voice sending them through dense woods and along fast-running creeks. They made it to the town in a little over an hour and a half.

The first cemetery was close to the college campus. West State Street Cemetery. The robot voice said, *"You have reached your destination."* In Audrina's opinion, the West State graveyard wasn't anything special. It looked no different than the Catholic cemetery in their own town—flat green lawn, recent headstones gleaming in the sunshine. The second was past the business district, close to the edge of town and the state forest park. This one was Zion Creek. Rolling slopes. A few ponds. Benches where Audrina sat with Damian and played slap-hands until Cat and Helen had had their fill of the century-old markers. After the third cemetery, Mansfield Meadows, they went back to the campus area to shop and maybe grab a burrito.

At Athens Gifts, Damian bought two of the same pin—a pink-eyed albino bat—and gave one to Audrina. "Just for fun," he said. Cat watched the whole exchange and secretly batted her eyelashes at her. Audrina blushed and shoved the pin into the pocket of her jean jacket.

The fourth cemetery was the most intriguing yet. It was the small graveyard located in the highlands west of town, on the grounds of a derelict psychiatric hospital called the Ridges, the main hall of which had recently been turned into an arts center. In the parking lot, Audrina and Damian stared in awe at the imposing brick structure. Of course, Helen felt the need to give them a history lesson about the architecture.

The burial ground for residents who'd died here was located around back. To reach it, you had to follow a path around the building, to the border of a cultivated copse of trees. The graves there were small, and some of them only had numbers engraved on them, which made Audrina feel sad.

"Look at these." Damian waved Audrina toward a collection of stones that were a bit larger than the rest. She bent to observe the names and dates. *EMMA. DAGMAR. NASH. DAISY. CLARK. MAXINE. PETER. CLAUDE. GARRETT. TOMMY. HEATHER.* No last names were listed. And none appeared to have lived past the age of fourteen.

"*Kids* stayed here?" Audrina asked Helen.

Helen checked out the stones. "Huh," she said. "I guess so."

"What's *this* supposed to mean?" Cat was crouched in shadow by a couple graves that were almost totally obscured by vines. The others went to see what she'd found. On the largest marker, instead of a name, a poem had been etched:

> Their skin is made of rotting leaves.
> Their bones are made of sticks.
> Their hair is moss and twine and string,
> Their voice, bat song and cricket clicks.

"This is creepy as heck," whispered Damian. Audrina agreed. She wanted to loop her arm around his, but she couldn't bear another lash-batting from her older sister.

"Check out *this* one," said Helen, stepping farther into the grove.

The final stone didn't even have a name. It simply read THE VOID. And an inscription: WHAT CAN ONE SAY ABOUT THE VOID THAT HASN'T ALREADY NOT BEEN SAID?

Cat chuckled, but Helen crossed her arms and shivered.

At the car, shadows stretched long upon the parking lot pavement. Cat started the engine and entered the address for the fifth cemetery into the GPS device. The robot voice spoke up, telling them loudly which way to go.

As Cat drove, Helen stared silently out the window. From the back seat, Audrina watched the girl's worried reflection and wondered if Helen really—*truly*—believed herself to be psychic. She wasn't sure what that even meant. For the first time that day, she felt glad she didn't know what Helen seemed to know.

"*In one thousand feet, turn right,*" said the robot voice. Cat paused at a stoplight, then followed the instructions. Along the curb, a spiked black iron fence lined an expansive field where gravestones poked up at strange angles. At the top of the hill, by an arch over a wide, paved path, the voice said, "*You have reached your destination.*" A sign told them they'd found Gate Cemetery, the last on Helen's list.

As Cat tried to parallel park, Helen spoke up. "Wait." She was peering through the windshield, into the growing dark. The sun had set and daylight was becoming scarce. She was focused on a structure down the slope a short distance—the white dome of a small intricately decorated chapel that reflected the purplish twilight.

"What's wrong?" asked Cat.

Damian raised an eyebrow at Audrina. She grimaced and bit at her lip.

"I don't want to go in there," Helen whispered.

"Why not?"

"It feels . . . *not right.*"

"Didn't we come here to see ghosts?" Audrina asked from the back seat. "There's something inherently *not right* about that."

Helen shook her head. "Let's just leave. Please."

At this, Audrina's skin puckered into gooseflesh. She stared at the white chapel down the slope, and suddenly, she too felt odd. It was as if the building were trying to . . . speak to her.

Cat sighed. "It's getting dark anyway. Mom might start to worry."

"So we're *not* going to see a ghost," Damian confirmed.

It felt suddenly clear to Audrina that none of them had actually believed they would.

"Let's hope that's the case," Cat answered cheerily, then pressed a button on her father's device, the one preset with directions for HOME.

"*Head straight*," said the robot voice. Cat pulled away from the curb. As they drove down the hill, Audrina noticed Helen watching the spire of the white chapel disappear behind the tree line.

The next intersection looked familiar. They'd passed by earlier on the way to one of the other cemeteries. Audrina knew the road out of town would be a few blocks to their left. But the robot voice instructed them to "*turn right*" instead. Cat listened, bringing them onto a dark street that went on for almost a half mile. At the next stop sign, the voice said "*turn right*" again. This new road was a steep slope upward, and as they went under a streetlamp, moving beyond some dense woods, that familiar iron fence appeared at the curb again.

They had circled Gate Cemetery and had stumbled upon its far side.

The car's gears groaned. Several hundred feet up the slope, the engine sputtered and died. Cat pulled the emergency brake, then whispered to herself, "What the..."

Beside the car, there was a small door in the fence. A chain looped through a hasp, but it hung loosely, unlocked. Someone had left the door open.

Helen inhaled a quick breath. Her eyes were fixed on a spot in the distance, just past the bump of a hill. The spire of the white chapel knifed up at the darkening sky. "Go, Cat," she said. "Hurry."

Cat twisted the key. The engine whined, then caught and growled back to life. She gunned the gas, but the vehicle wouldn't budge.

"Hurry!"

Cat groaned and released the brake. They all flew back against the seats as the car shot forward, up, over the crest, then zoomed down the other side. Audrina held her palms against the ceiling, trying to steady herself. Damian looked terrified. Frantic, Helen pressed at the HOME button on the GPS device.

When they made it to the next intersection, the voice repeated, *"turn right."* Gate Cemetery's iron fence remained beside them. The GPS seemed to want them to circle it. Audrina was glad they could no longer see any part of that weird white chapel. Around the corner, the device said again, *"turn right."* The car was now back on the road that they'd left only minutes ago, heading up toward the cemetery gate once more. Helen gripped the handle over the passenger side door, her knuckles white.

Cat tapped at the black box, annoyed. "This thing must be messed up." She was trying to sound rational, ignoring Helen's radiating fear.

When they reached the top of the hill where the archway opened onto the path through the gravestones, the robot voice once more blurted out, *"turn right."*

Cat skidded the car to a stop. For a few seconds, no one spoke. Audrina said what they were all thinking. "Does it want us to go in there?"

"I don't *care* what it wants!" Helen shouted. "Move, Cat! Now!"

Cat pressed the gas pedal. The tires whined and spun. At the bottom of the same hill, the dang robot voice told them to turn right again.

So Cat turned left.

By the time they reached the road that led out of town, the GPS device seemed to have reset itself and offered helpful suggestions for how to get where they needed to be. The group slowly reset itself too, calmer now, chuckling about what had just happened. Audrina thought it was hilarious when Helen started going on about how cool the experience at the fifth cemetery had been. How it was proof that the legend of the five cemeteries was real, that she *really* was a psychic medium and could feel things *deeply*. Audrina kept to herself that she'd also sensed a strangeness there, that it would have been a bad idea to pull through the gate and head down that path, but this was suddenly all about Helen, and how Helen was the special one, and how *Helen* had saved the day.

Damian rolled his eyes and smiled, which made Audrina smile too. When you go through something like what they'd just gone through together, it had to bring you closer, right? He took the albino bat pin from his pocket and attached it to the lapel of his Members Only jacket. He held out his palm to Audrina and asked where she'd put hers. When she handed it to him, he removed the backing and pushed the pin through Audrina's jacket too. "There," he said. "Now we're the same."

The road through the dark hills was lulling, and despite Helen's mixtape blasting from the front speakers, Audrina found herself dozing. Every now and again, the robot voice from the black box would rouse and speak some new direction, but mostly she settled into the plush seat.

Soon, familiar houses moved across her vision. Cat had finally made it back to their neighborhood.

From the stereo, Blondie was singing, *"One way . . . or another."*

Ahead, their driveway appeared.

"Turn right," said the voice from the box. Audrina sighed. Couldn't they have shut off the annoying thing already?

Cat used the turn signal, which ticked like the second hand of a clock, then she swung the wheel to the right. The car bumped slightly as it crossed the low curb. But then, everything changed.

They weren't at their house.

They were heading down a dark path.

Confused, Audrina looked out the rear window. Behind them, an iron arch reached over an open gate. The grass on either side of the car was marred with headstones, tilting every which way. "Cat?" she called out. "Where are we?"

But Cat didn't answer. Helen sat in the passenger seat staring straight ahead. Debbie Harry crooned from the radio that she was gonna *get ya, get ya, get ya, get ya.*

The car jostled along the path, heading down a slope into a darkness that gathered more densely the farther they traveled.

When Damian slipped his hand into hers and gave it a squeeze, she only felt annoyed. "Where *are* we?" Again, no one answered, but Damian squeezed her hand tighter, as if in reassurance.

More gravestones flashed in her side vision, the car's headlights ricocheting off them like mirrors. A knot tied up Audrina's stomach. She remembered the names of the children she'd seen on the markers behind the "lunatic asylum." And that weird poem. And THE VOID.

What can one say about THE VOID . . .

All of it was adding up to something Audrina felt on the verge of understanding.

Cat hit the brakes.

The seat belt caught Audrina's shoulder. Frozen in the headlights ahead, a building rose from a vast field. White marble curved up into a dome that narrowed into a spire. The chapel. Gate Cemetery. The place that had scared the pants off Helen. Now Helen didn't seem to notice; she stared forward as if unseeing. Or *uncaring*. The chapel's white double doors opened inward, revealing shadows so dark, they looked almost solid.

Damian's squeezing grew even tighter.

So tight, Audrina felt the bones in her hand start to go out of joint.

She jerked away from his grip, ready to let him have it. This was no time for teasing!

Turning, she found a hulking figure in the center seat.

Beyond, Damian was leaning against the other door, snoring.

Unable to catch her breath, Audrina looked up at the shape, whose head pressed against the car's ceiling, its neck tilting at an impossible angle. The thing stared back, white eyes gleaming like headlights. She flailed for the door handle, but it wouldn't budge.

The voice from the box spoke one last time. *"YOU'VE REACHED YOUR DESTINATION."*

GILBERT CHANGES TRAINS

The station announcement blurted from the speakers overhead, shocking Gilbert back into his body. He stopped the tape, then scrambled out of the car before the doors slid shut behind him and the train pulled away.

As the platform emptied around him, the stories flickered in his memory. Gilbert felt *off*. He checked his phone. This station was a decent ways from where he'd gotten on, and the tape had played for a long while. Yet, according to his phone, only a few minutes had passed since his last message to Percy.

Shaking it off as nerves, Gilbert made his way up the stairs and along the corridor, thinking of Ant, trying to remember the last conversation they'd had. Probably something stupid about video games. Gilbert hated to admit it, but he and Ant had never been very close. Was it that Ant was a few years older? Or maybe they were just different types of people. Ant was frequently insecure, secretive, quiet. Gilbert leaned on Percy's friendship, felt constantly curious, liked to try new things, and he often shared his enthusiasm with those he loved. Whatever the case, this day had only made Gilbert want to know his brother better—if they were both able to make it through . . .

On the platform, he looked to the darkened tunnel that would take him to Aunt Sheila and her oxtail stew and johnny-cakes. His mouth watered, but he wasn't sure his rumbling stomach would keep anything down. He couldn't stop imagining Ant's face—cut up, bruised, covered in red.

But then, the train going in the *opposite* direction arrived. Without a second thought, Gilbert entered one of those cars instead.

> I'm heading to you.

> ...

> I thought your grandma wanted you at your aunt's?

> Something weird's going on. I need your help to figure it out.

> ...

> Why?

> Hard to explain. More when I get there.

The subway doors slid shut.

> OK. I'll be here.

Grandma Rosemary would be furious. But this was more important. The tapes felt like a key that might save his brother. If he could figure out what they were telling him. And what secrets they held.

The train squealed as it hugged a sharp curve and turned south.

On the wall across the car, Gilbert noticed odd graffiti. It reminded him of the **O** he'd seen on the table at the hospital, marked in the same thick ink and in a similar style. But instead of a single **O**, now there were three, plus an **N**.

NO   OO

An idea struck Gilbert. The first **O** had appeared after he'd listened to the story in the cafeteria—"Exterminators." Then, riding on the green line, he'd listened to three more tales. And now, somehow, three more letters had appeared.

A coincidence?

Something told him this was because of the tapes, or because of him *listening* to the tapes. In a way, it felt like the tales were *warping* the world. Changing Gilbert's . . . *reality*. Or maybe . . . his *mind*?

On closer inspection, Gilbert noticed four small drawings surrounding the letters. One was a crate that looked like it might contain a monster. Another was a spiky seashell. A third was a charm shaped like a hand. The fourth was a detailed illustration of a chapel. Gilbert realized that each one corresponded with a story from the tape.

NO   OO

He understood suddenly: *This* was why Ant had told him to not listen. The tapes *were* a key . . . to something strange and beyond his comprehension. By listening, had he just turned it in a lock?

If so, did that mean he *should not* continue?

Gilbert sat again and thought of Ant, unconscious in the hospital bed, desperate for a cure.

Of course he *should*.

CREEP CASTLE

B**owen's** Land of Amusement had stood along the sandy coast in the suburbs south of the city for almost fifty years. No one knew why the owners hadn't reopened the park for the past three summers.

Already, the grounds were shabby. Weeds and vines had cracked the concrete path. Colors had faded on the rides that peeked up over the park's fence—the carousel with the metal flag, the spiderweb Ferris wheel, the fun house like a gothic castle. Its turret had marked the highest point of the park before a freak storm had toppled the tip a few seasons back.

Some people suspected the storm damage had been more extensive than the Bowens had reported. There were rumors the family had let their insurance lapse. Others conjectured darker reasons for the closure, but that talk was quieter—whispered in high-school hallways, written in cryptic messages on walls in public bathrooms on the boardwalk—easily dismissed if ever the question of the family's history were raised. The locals still held hope for a return to normalcy. Though the beaches nearby continued to bring in tourists by the busload, the town had suffered from the loss of their prized attraction, and not only financially.

Once, it had been a kind of rite for the local teens to work at the Land of Amusement during school breaks—a way to keep out of trouble, and also to find it. Lately, visiting the abandoned park after sunset had become a new rite—a secret that young people worked hard to keep.

One early September evening, two boys made their way toward the border fence around the corner from the gate. They dropped their bikes behind some overgrown box hedges. The air was humid, and there was a rare stillness from the ocean. The sound of waves was ever present in this area, but today, the water slid gently upon the shore, almost as softly as the breeze.

Garrett was fourteen years old. Claude was thirteen. They'd met at church camp earlier that summer. Garrett's father was the priest of the Episcopal congregation just down the street.

Claude's family was a new arrival—both to the church and to the town. After Claude's grandmother Millie had moved into a nursing home that spring, they'd taken up residence in her house, a Queen Anne Victorian, not unlike many of the run-down homes in the area.

The church camp had been poorly attended, with few kids Claude's age. So when Garrett had asked Claude to hang out, of course he'd said yes. Over the past few weeks, they'd spent days at the beach—bodysurfing, biking the boardwalk, throwing small stones at hungry seagulls. Claude thought this last part was slightly cruel, but when Garrett's poor aim made him miss the birds, he figured it was okay to try and miss them too.

This was the end of their first full week of school. There were big personalities in Claude's eighth-grade class, so he'd stayed quiet, slunk through the shadows, tried to remain unseen. At lunch Garrett noticed Claude acting withdrawn, so to cheer him up, he'd promised a surprise if Claude came to his house around 6:00 p.m. Dinner was hot dogs and corn on the cob.

Then, as the sun dipped lower, they'd snuck off on their bikes.

"You've got to get down lower," Garrett whispered from inside the border fence. "Like a snake."

Claude crawled through the gap. He'd been inside amusement parks before, but he'd never seen one lit only by the glow of twilight and stars. At the midway, Garrett waved for Claude to follow. Silhouettes of shuttered kiosks lined the route toward the carousel. Trash bins had been knocked over, litter strewn around. Garrett had brought a couple flashlights, but he didn't turn them on yet. "Would be like setting off an alarm if anyone catches a glimpse."

What if someone caught them? How would their parents respond? "You said you had a surprise," Claude mentioned as they passed the carousel and ventured farther into the park.

"Being here with me isn't a big enough surprise for you?"

"I mean, yeah. Sure. This is really . . . fun."

Garrett chuckled. "I'm saving the best part for when we get in *there*." He pointed ahead, toward the looming silhouette of a large building that looked like a fortress. "Creep Castle."

Claude swallowed what little saliva was left in his mouth.

"Scared?" Garrett teased.

"Should I be?"

Garrett shrugged and walked on, leaving Claude alone to consider the answer.

Up close, it was clear that the building's dimensions were deceiving—forced perspective made the castle appear larger than it actually was. An empty moat surrounded its base. Garrett strolled purposefully across a small bridge and through a tall doorway. "You coming?" he asked, flicking on his flashlight finally. He tossed the other to Claude, who fumbled it, nearly dropping it into the moat.

"Is this safe?"

"Sure," Garrett answered. "Why wouldn't it be?"

Together, the boys stepped into darkness.

At the end of May, when Claude's parents had told him they were moving into Millie's house, he'd felt a swarm of emotions.

Part of him was excited to live in such a grand abode. He'd always been fond of Grandma Millie, as well as the house that her own parents had left to her. The place had a particular scent that made him feel cozy and warm, something that brought him back to when he was little and Millie would have him sit at the kitchen table and mix brownie batter, when they'd play hide-and-seek in the cavernous basement, or sit on the couch in the den and read picture books to each other.

Another part of him was angry with his parents. Millie was still alive, and though she needed full-time care, the house still belonged to her. When they'd arrived and Millie was no longer there, Claude felt like they'd betrayed her, especially when his parents carted her belongings off to storage. He understood that the decision to get Millie the help she needed had been difficult for everyone. Dad had explained that since Millie's house was closer to the nursing home than theirs had been, the change would be for the best. Here, they could visit Millie every day and attend to her many needs.

Creep Castle clearly didn't have anyone attending to its needs. Claude swung his flashlight every which way, careful to avoid the debris scattered in the slim twisted passage—broken chairs, smashed lightbulbs, picture frames with slashed canvases. There was even a baby carriage, tipped over on its side.

"Some jerks made a mess," said Garrett.

Millie popped into Claude's mind—thoughts of how his parents had moved her belongings without her permission. But this place was unlike Millie's house. Here, the walls were black. There were no windows. Even during daytime, sunlight could not sneak inside.

"Where are we going?"

"You'll see," said Garrett, holding the light under his chin.

When Claude stepped into the next space, he yelped. Standing just out of sight, Garrett had focused his beam on someone across a ballroom. Garrett heaved a laugh. Claude gritted his teeth. The person across the room didn't move, and he realized they were part of the decor. "Not funny," he said. He illuminated the figure. It was dressed in a fancy Victorian-style tuxedo and a cape with a high collar. Its arms crisscrossed its chest. Its sneer revealed long fangs, glistening red.

Garrett crossed the wide room. "This guy used to race toward you when your group entered." He tapped the floor with his toe. "There's a track here. See?" Curious, Claude followed. A groove marked the wood like a scar. Garrett lit the vampire's pockmarked and rubbery gray skin. "He would have reached out for a hug." He pulled at the vampire's arms, trying to extend them. "Mechanical. See?" In the dark, Claude thought the vampire's expression might have changed—its brow furrowing, its black eyes shining briefly. Garrett gave the bent arms a yank. The vampire jerked forward. Claude leaped back with another yelp.

Dislodged from the track, the thing knocked Garrett aside and then hit the floor with a bang.

The boys' mouths dropped open. Garrett let out another laugh. Claude couldn't help but join in. Uneasy chortles bounced around the space. "We're going to get in so much trouble!"

"Are we, though?" Garrett asked, stepping toward another dark doorway.

Claude crouched to examine the vampire. A piece of its face had broken off, revealing wires and tubes and bolts and a bent metal frame. One of the fangs had chipped. Strangely, the thought of his grandmother—lying in bed at the nursing home—swept down upon him, sending him scrambling after his friend.

The second floor was a series of crowded dioramas featuring classic movie monsters—rotting zombies in one room, an Egyptian mummy in the next, ghosts wearing sheets in a third, even some kind of man-fish hybrid, all scales and claws and barnacles. Thankfully, there were plenty of doors marked EXIT.

Garrett didn't glance at Claude when he sat beside him. "Pretty cool, right?" A dim flame flickered at Garrett's fingertips.

It took Claude a moment to realize his friend was holding a silver flip lighter, embossed with a grinning skull. "Where'd you get that?"

"Stole it from a kid at school."

"Hard-core." The most Claude had ever stolen was a late-night cookie from the kitchen.

"Check this out." Garrett held up what looked like a belt. A string with little red tubes attached to it. He must have been hiding it in his pocket. His lighter sparked the string. Giddy, Garrett tossed the belt thing to the floor. Before Claude could move, the room was filled with noise and light and smoke.

Snap! Bang! Crack! Blam!

Claude covered his ears, closed his eyes, tucked into a ball.

The commotion stopped as quickly as it had begun.

Of course, Garrett was laughing again. "Surprise!"

"Wh-what surprise?" Claude asked, choking on sulfurous fumes.

"*That* was your surprise. Did you like it?"

"Did I like almost getting blown to smithereens?" Claude almost lashed out, yelled that *NO, HE DIDN'T LIKE IT*, but something in his brain shifted, and he realized . . . "That *was* pretty amazing." He let out a coughing chuckle. "Where'd you get firecrackers?"

"They were left over from some summer celebration my dad had in the church parking lot. He has no idea I took them."

Claude waved his hand to clear away the smoke. The fish-man was glaring down at them. Had its mouth opened wider since they'd first arrived? "It's hot in here. Can we go?"

Garrett held out another string. "We can. After *you* give it a shot."

Claude took the lighter. The firecrackers too. His nerves made him shiver. It was one thing to watch but another to light the fuse himself. Garrett looked impatient, so Claude flipped the lid and flicked the button.

This time, the explosives detonated immediately.

Shocked, Claude tossed the belt away from himself.

Snap! Bang! Crack! Blam!

He jumped up as sparks bounced off the fish-man's scaly calves and thighs, skittering around the room.

Garrett grabbed Claude's arm. "Come on!" He shoved at one of the EXIT doors and dragged Claude onto a fire escape. Outside, he gulped down breath after cool breath.

"Hurry!" Garrett called, taking off down the rusting steps.

When the boys reached the bridge over the moat and looked up, Claude felt dizzy. Smoke billowed out of the broken turret.

"We've gotta split." They ran down the midway, past the darkened food kiosks and game stations, toward the alley and the fence from which they'd come. Garrett kicked at the top edge of the hole, breaking away chunks of wood, making the gap wider. A moment later, the boys were outside. They bolted for their bikes. "Go home!" Garrett yelled as his tires spun out on the street.

Claude gawped after him. Not knowing what else to do, he kicked off toward Millie's place alone.

Later, after the sirens ended, after his parents had come back inside and stopped wondering aloud what could be going on, after he'd gone up to his bedroom, complaining of a headache, Claude phoned Garrett's house.

"It's a little late," Garrett's father said after Claude asked to speak with his son.

"I'm sorry, Father Josh. I need to ask Garrett something real quick."

When Garrett picked up, he sounded panicked. "Are you nuts? Calling here?"

"I wanted to check . . . Have you heard anything?"

"About what?"

"About—"

"*No*," Garrett interrupted. "We were never there. Got it?"

For a moment, Claude's voice stopped working. Garrett had never spoken to him like this before. Heat ignited inside his ribs. "What we did was wrong, Garrett."

"What *you* did, you mean?"

So that's how it's going to be? "We should tell someone."

"Why would you even think that?"

"I feel bad."

"Oh, you *feel bad*? Take some Alka-Seltzer!" Garrett breathed into the receiver. "Look, I'm sorry you feel this way. And yes, what happened was not . . . good. But you have no idea what would happen to me . . . to *us* . . . if anyone found out. Get it? Creep Castle is gone. I've already got two strikes with my parents this year." What was that supposed to mean? Claude thought of the vampire's face—the real one made of metal and wires, hidden under the rubber mask. "If you tell . . . you'll regret it."

Funny, thought Claude. *I already regret everything.*
You especially.

Claude hung up, missing his Millie more than ever. His family lived close enough to visit her every day now. Why didn't they?

He stretched out on his mattress, feeling so very small.

As he slowly willed himself to sleep, he imagined the creatures from the castle. How, as the place went up around them, their glass eyes reflected that blazing light. Orange against black. How, if only for a moment, it appeared as though they'd been sparked with life.

You *are lying on the dusty floor of an old ballroom, looking through eyes you haven't used in a long time.*

The room is slowly filling up with smoke, obscuring the already dim walls. Creaking, cracking sounds come from above.

Then there are footsteps. Hands pull you up, steady you. A strange kind of light appears—an orange, dancing glow that filters through thick air.

You glance at the group surrounding you. They stare, unsure that you're as capable as they are. All are familiar. You came from the same place, long ago. The bosses gave you all the same tasks: to move when instructed, bare your teeth, reach out your long gray fingers, display your nails like a threat, make the people who visit your castle shriek with terror and amazement.

A powerful sensation envelops you. If you could feel pain, you would recognize it as such. Glancing down, you see that the dancing glow clings to your long black cloak, your tuxedo, your skin.

This is fire, you think. Those children brought it to your home.

The group waves for you to follow. Your mechanical legs are stiff. You understand that the group wishes to return this glowing light—the fire—to those who gifted it. One by one, the group disappears through an open door, each of them dressed in this strange light. There is the man who is green and scaly, and the few whose flesh was bruised and rotting even before the flickering glow began to turn them black, and the woman who was made almost entirely of dust and wrapped in bandages that now billow and break apart in the wavering heat.

You exit into a wide expanse—a dark world whose ceiling is so tall, no one could ever reach it, speckled with pinprick radiance that makes you think of the place you were created—and onto a strange path through a landscape that is utterly alien.

Ahead, there are flashing lights, different from the glow that flickers around you and your friends. These new lights are red, white, blue. A screaming fills the space between them. Sirens?

At the end of this path is a gate. Its doors crash open. The flashing grows brighter, the screaming louder. A monstrous vehicle rushes toward you, and you see that this is where it's all coming from—the lights, the noise. Another vehicle follows the first. And another. Like a parade. A celebration.

The man—green and scaly—is quick. He guides your group into a pocket of shadow as the vehicles rumble by. Looking back, you see the castle where you've spent most of your life, doing what you've been told. The glowing—the flames—have engulfed its silhouette, creating a shimmer so bright it is blinding to behold. Overhead, a shadow billows, up and up and up, obscuring those twinkling pinpricks embedded in the impossibly tall ceiling. You all make your way down a new path, hidden now from the people who are dressed in strange armor, who are shouting and lugging weapons with which they mean to battle the dancing glow.

Stepping out onto a stone plaza—cracked, scattered with stones, littered with broken glass, tall grasses wavering—you notice that the glowing has engulfed almost your entire body. You don't have much time. But you carry on after the others.

The farther you go, the less sure you are of the world around you. When you left the room that you knew, things changed. And the more you consider that tall ceiling, the more certain you are that it's not a ceiling at all. No. This is what is called outside.

There is a kind of freedom here. You feel a new spark inside you. Different from the glowing, the flames, the fire, the gift.

You walk by buildings and vehicles and . . . What is the word? Trees. Giant branches waving back and forth as if cheering you and your friends onward. You can do it! You're almost there!

Ahead, you see a house. A big house. Fanciful embellishments decorate its exterior. Electric light spills from glass bulbs by a grand door. This is the place. The boy who brought you this gift of glow and escape—who planted this wondrous spark, this change you never knew was possible—is inside. You're not sure how, but you know it's true.

Some of your group has fallen behind, so bright now, they struggle to continue. But you force yourself to walk, to keep up with the man—green and scaly. Together, you mark the fresh lawn with black footsteps. The ground smolders where heat threatens to bloom. Together you climb the stairs, holding the wooden banister to keep your balance. Once you've made it to the doorway, the man—green and scaly and blackened—gestures at a button attached to the wall. You extend a finger, which looks different now. Your insides have found their way outside. You depress the button with a newly sharp and metallic claw.

Inside a bell rings.

Rings.

Rings.

Rings.

The dancing glow climbs the walls, licks at the roof over the porch.

Voices shout from behind the door.

The man—green and scaly and blackened—directs your group to the yard, between the trees, where your heat makes leaves whip in a frenzy.

You watch a family bolt from the house. Two grown-ups and a child. The boy who brought the gift. They're too taken by the blaze to notice your hiding place.

The father runs to the neighbors as the mom and the boy watch. The blaze moves quickly. Now the wraparound porch is a gleaming rampart. It reaches up to the second story. The boy holds his mother's hand as she cries. The night is quiet, but the dancing glow makes its own kind of noise.

Gets louder.

Louder.

Lights blink on in adjacent houses, people who've come

to see the spectacle, just like how those crowds used to come to your home to see you. A wailing rises up, shatters the air. Those sirens. Heading this way now.

The boy is staring at you. He breaks away from his mother. Steps toward your spot between the trees, where your own glow is fading finally. "Garrett?" he calls out. "Is that you?"

Excitement buzzes your body. Or maybe it's electricity?

"Did you do this?" the boy shouts as his mother pulls him back. "I'll regret it? That's what you said?"

This isn't right. The boy is upset. This was not supposed to happen.

Gifts are meant to make one happy.

You feel the others fretting. They widen the circle. Sensing trouble. As if about to run. You remember that your bosses can be cruel.

The boy crosses the lawn, ignoring the blackened prints you've left behind. His footfalls crunch carefully through dead brush. In the shadows, he squints. "I can see you, Garrett." Full of confidence, the boy enters the clearing, pausing when he notices the smoldering ground. The brush by your feet is ready to ignite. His small eyes reflect the new glowing. Orange against black. A spark of life.

Your friends sidle behind him, closing the circle. He spins, taking you in, his mouth dropping open in awe. "What's this?" he asks. His mother calls to him from in the yard, but he ignores her. "Who are you?"

Darkness billows up from the ground. The flickering grows again. The boy tries to run, but you hold up your hands to keep him here.

He's asked you a question: Who are you?

How satisfying it is to give him an answer.

DUMMY

Daisy Jackson wouldn't have been out biking after dark if not for the story Clark Kowalski had shared with her and Maxine Kim during lunch that day. He'd heard it from his father, the police chief, earlier in the week:

About a month back, Officer Mannis had pulled over some rando and discovered his pickup's bed filled with dirt. When Mannis dug down several inches, he found hundreds, maybe thousands, of earthworms, burrowing through the soil. At the station, the driver had argued, almost violently, that he hadn't broken any laws. Mannis hated when citizens spoke up, so out of spite, he'd waited a long while before allowing the man to make a call. By the time an elderly woman arrived to drive the man to his truck and the bed of worms, he'd begun shouting about *curses* and *messing with the wrong people*. The experience made Mannis recall tales he'd heard as a child, about a family of witches who lived in the woods over the hill, several miles past Upper Yarrow Road.

This alone was strange, Clark had explained, but as he went on, it got stranger.

See, a few years back, the police station had set up a mannequin, dressed in the uniform of the local force, along with a metal stand that held a placard reading HOW MAY I BE OF SERVICE? The mannequin's face was all white—no eyes, nose, or mouth. The local teens called the creepy thing Officer Dummy.

Since Mannis's encounter with the worm-man, there'd been odd occurrences at the station. Sometimes, in the mornings, the staff would find Officer Dummy facing a corner, or standing behind the HOW MAY I BE OF SERVICE? placard, or even lying facedown under the lighting fixture in the middle of the lobby. Mannis believed they'd all been cursed, but Clark's dad scoffed at the idea that it was anything but a prank.

Prank or curse, Clark was curious to figure it out, either way. When he suggested a visit to the station, Daisy had said, "I'm not sure it's a good idea to mess with the police."

"We wouldn't be *messing* with anyone. We'd simply be checking to see if the stories are true. Besides, I know everyone there. My dad's chief, remember?"

"Well, I'm curious as heck," Maxine replied. "I say we do it. *Tonight.*"

Now Daisy weaved her way through side streets toward Maxine's neighborhood, which was only a few blocks from the police station. The air was cool, and she wished she'd worn a warmer jacket.

Maxine and Clark straddled their bikes at the end of Maxine's long driveway. "Yo!" Maxine said as Daisy approached. "You ready for this?"

"Probably not," Daisy answered. "Is it dumb that I'm actually kind of freaked out?"

"That's the whole point," whispered Clark. "Witches and curses and faceless mannequins pretending to be cops? It is *our duty* to freak out." He adjusted the straps of his backpack. "I've got our supplies. Binoculars. Polaroid. Deer jerky." Daisy cringed, imagining Chief Kowalski prepping the meat in his basement.

Having moved recently from the city, Daisy's experience with cops was different than that of her new friends. Clark's and Maxine's parents had most certainly never talked with them about how to handle an encounter with the law—*especially* Clark, who always seemed so sure of himself and his own safety. Being a son of THE LAW had its privileges.

Still, the three had bonded over other things.

Scary things.

On the first day of school, Maxine had observed Daisy at a lunch table in the corner, devouring a Stephen King novel. "My mom won't let me read books like this," she'd said, in awe of Daisy's daring. Minutes later, she introduced Daisy to Clark. He'd told her about his secret collection of VHS horror tapes that he kept in a box under his bed. His favorites were

A Nightmare on Elm Street and *Halloween*. Daisy admitted she was more of a *Poltergeist* and *Monster Squad* kind of kid. Maxine loved *Alien* and *Aliens* and other stuff with action, spaceships, and girls who knew how to kick butt.

When the trio reached the police station, they laid their bikes beyond the curb across the street. The orange glow of streetlights illuminated the damp air of the nearly empty parking lot, making the world look slightly out of focus. They sat in the grass between the street and the woods. Through the large windows, Daisy noticed the metal stand and the famous placard that read HOW MAY I BE OF SERVICE?

"Where's Officer Dummy?" asked Maxine, holding the binoculars.

"It's supposed to stand beside the placard," said Clark.

Daisy scanned the room. Through an opening in the wall, she noticed a woman at a desk, reading or writing. But the mannequin was not to be seen.

"It moved already," Clark whispered. He scrambled for the compact Polaroid, then snapped a shot of the nothingness that existed beside the sign, as if a photo of a deserted police station lobby would be proof.

"If we wait long enough, maybe it'll come back," Maxine suggested.

Daisy wondered if they'd come up here for nothing. She had to admit, however, that hiding in the dark, spying on things that might or might not exist, was kind of fun. She'd never have been able to do this down in the city without worrying some stranger might step out of the shadows.

A dog barked somewhere down the hill.

"Who is that?" asked Clark.

Daisy thought he meant the dog. But no—someone stood still under one of the streetlights in the station's parking lot. Daisy reached for the binoculars. Through the lens, it looked like they wore a police uniform.

"Lemme see," Clark said, grabbing the binoculars.

"They're not moving," said Maxine. "Like, at all."

"Are they watching us?" Daisy asked. "Is it an officer?"

"I can't tell," said Clark. He raised the Polaroid again, covering the flashbulb, snapping another shot. By now, the first one was almost developed. "Creeping crud." He showed it to the girls. "Look at this." In the photo of the lobby, in the space by the placard where there'd been nothing, an indistinct figure had appeared. Blue jacket. Blue pants. The blur of a cap on top of what might have been a head. "This wasn't there when I took the picture."

"It definitely was not," Maxine agreed.

"Guys," Daisy said. "The person is gone."

In the lot, the silhouette had disappeared.

Worry crinkled Maxine's brow. "Maybe it was just a cop? Maybe they went into the station?"

"I didn't hear the door open," said Clark.

"We weren't paying attention," Maxine retorted.

It felt safer to believe the simple explanation.

When the sound of a stick snapping rang out from the trees behind them, all three flinched and turned. The station's lights barely reached here, but as Daisy's eyes adjusted, it became clear that someone was standing there, inside a clump of saplings.

Clark choked out, "Hello?"

"Who's there?" asked Maxine.

There was a shifting of weight, the sound of crunching leaves.

"I'm Clark Kowalski," Clark went on, daring to stand. "My dad's the chief."

No answer came from within the trees.

Maxine stood too. "Don't screw with us. We know how to fight!"

"*Maxine*," Daisy whispered. She lifted her bike from the ground. "We've got some evidence," she said, nodding at the camera strapped at Clark's wrist. "Let's go." The others didn't need convincing. Within seconds they were flying down the street toward Maxine's house.

Ahead, a figure blocked the road—the same silhouette they'd seen in the parking lot. The three skidded to a stop. The person didn't move—just watched, looking very much like a mannequin.

But how'd Officer Dummy get out here? Unless someone was messing with them?

Without thinking, Daisy did a U-turn and headed up the hill instead. Her thighs screamed as she tried to make her bike go faster, but it felt like she was moving through mud. Her friends followed closely, their tires kicking up dust.

As the road ascended into the hills, the buildings were few and far between, but if they continued on, in about a half mile, it should emerge by the baseball fields near the middle school. For nearly a minute, they raced into almost total darkness.

At the next streetlight, they paused to catch their breath. A low mist blanketed the ground. "It might have been nothing," Daisy said, trying to answer their unspoken question. "We were at the police station. Maybe we saw *the police*?"

Clark shook his head. "They don't act like that. They *know* me."

Daisy rolled her eyes before she could stop herself, hoping he hadn't noticed. When a siren whooped from up the hill, a single high-pitched blare, she almost fell off her bike.

There was a swirl of lights, red and blue—a police car parked near the curb. The driver's door opened. Someone stepped out and directed a flashlight in their direction. Daisy held up a hand to block the glare. "What are you kids doing out here?" a deep voice called.

Clark spoke up. "We're riding our bikes."

There was a pause, and the voice said, "Clark? Is that you?"

Daisy felt herself come back to her body.

"Yes. I'm sorry, sir. Is there a problem?"

The officer lowered the flashlight and walked over. "We've been getting calls about a big animal heading through some folks' backyards. A bear, maybe. It's not safe." He waved them forward. "Hop in. I'll give you all a ride home."

"What about our bikes?" Clark asked.

"I'll come back for them later. Swing by the station tomorrow."

As she laid her bike in a pile of dead leaves, Daisy grew nervous. She didn't know what her parents would think if they saw a cop car pull into their driveway. Climbing into the back seat, she figured it would be better than getting eaten by a bear. She shuffled toward the far door. Maxine followed. Clark entered last. The officer closed them inside.

It had all happened so fast, Daisy had almost forgotten what they'd been racing from. The silhouette of a mannequin that moved by itself? A possible witch's curse? *Ridiculous*, she told herself as the officer jostled behind the wheel. *You've seen too many scary movies.*

"What's your name, officer?" asked Clark.

"Bowen," the man answered without looking back.

Daisy realized that she hadn't gotten a good look at his face. From where she sat, she could only catch glimpses from the side. In the dashboard light, his nose was long and straight. He wore a short, dark mustache. His jawline was sharp, like a tough guy in a comic book.

"Officer Bowen?" Clark said. "I don't think we've met."

"I'm new," said the cop, shifting the car into drive, turning up the hill in the opposite direction from where they'd come. The momentum tossed Clark and Maxine into Daisy. She took one last look back at her bike at the side of the road, illuminated red, and knew that this whole thing had been a mistake.

"He's *new*?" she whispered.

Maxine scowled. Clark shrugged. But then the driver sped up, passed the turn toward the baseball fields, continued into the hills. "Excuse me, sir," said Clark, looping his fingers through the wire mesh that separated the front seats from the rear. "We live down *that* way."

The driver didn't look back. "Oh, didn't I say? I'd gotten a call. Some kids need help out at the reservoir. Should be a quick check-in."

"Can you just let us out?" Daisy asked. "We'll walk back to our bikes."

"Not with a potential mama bear out there. Sit tight. You'll be home in no time."

"Will you at least radio my dad?" Clark continued. "Let him know where we're at?"

"He knows where you're at," said the man.

That didn't sound right, but Clark gestured for everyone to chill. It amazed Daisy how much faith he could put in a complete stranger. She tugged at the door handle, but of course it was locked.

They rode along the winding roads that her father took to work each morning—miles and miles from where they'd started. Daisy's brain was in hyperdrive, backflipping around the patrol car's interior for a way to escape. A lose screw. A bent section of wire mesh. Space beneath the seats. She wondered how thick the windows were and how hard they might be to smash. Against the opposite door, Clark was peering out into the night, as if everything were fine. Beside her, Maxine sighed. "We need to make a plan," Daisy whispered.

"For what?" Maxine whispered back.

Daisy gave her a look like *REALLY?* What happened to the girl who kicked butt?

Daisy leaned forward. "Officer Bowen? Would you mind asking the station to tell my mom where I'm at?"

"Of course," said the driver. "Again, I'm real sorry about this. Kinda got mixed up here." He lifted the receiver, spoke to the dispatch desk: "Do me a favor and call the parents of these kids I got with me . . . Yep, Clark Kowalski, Maxine Kim, and Daisy Jackson. Thanks a bunch. Over and out." He tilted his head toward Daisy but didn't turn around. "Feel better now?"

How did he know her full name?

"Uh-huh," Daisy lied. No one on the other end had said a

word. She wasn't sure she'd even seen him press the button.

Maxine's expression now mirrored her own. This guy wasn't a cop. Was this even a real police car? *As soon as he opens the back door, we rush him. We run. We survive this.*

The driver made a turn onto a gravel service road. Potholes made the back seat jounce. Pine branches and scrub brush whipped the windows. The driver flipped a switch, and the lights flashed. When Daisy clutched at Maxine's hand, Clark noticed and tossed them a curious look. Over the crest of a small hill, a wide body of water appeared down a slight slope, its surface as black as night, except for stars reflected back at the sky.

"What kind of help do these kids at the reservoir need?" Daisy dared to ask.

Officer Bowen grunted. "Report was they're trapped in a car." He struck a deep divot and all three of them flew into the air. When they settled, the police car slowed. The water's edge was just ahead. The tires squeaked and crackled across a pebbly clearing, stopping with the front half of the vehicle reaching across the water line. There were no other cars parked nearby, no other kids in trouble.

Daisy squeezed Maxine's hand to grab her attention. *He opens the door, we rush him, we run—*

"Officer Bowen?" said Clark. "What are we doing?"

The cop was still now. Silent. The engine idled.

"Sir?" Clark tried again.

The officer let out a gritty chuckle.

"This isn't funny," said Maxine.

"Let us out," Daisy demanded.

"I can't," the officer whispered. He sounded different, as if he were speaking through a mouthful of earth. "There are kids out at the reservoir. Trapped in a car."

Daisy's skin went all gooseflesh. Had this been a joke? A trick? To teach them a lesson for riding their bikes after dark? Or maybe the officer was hazing the police chief's kid. Bragging rights?

He took his foot off the brake, and the car eased forward. Peering out the window, Daisy saw the water was at the bottom of the door.

"You can't do this to us," Clark said, finally aghast.

"Can't I?" the voice came again, more like the *idea* of a voice now. The officer pressed the gas, and the car moved into the water, catching the slope, pitching sharply. The hood submerged. Flashes of red, white, and blue flickered out into the surrounding darkness. The headlights cast two beams down, down, down. Water was seeping through the seams around the doors.

The officer opened the windows a crack, and the lake began to quickly fill the car.

There was screaming. Pounding at the glass.

More and more water came.

The officer edged farther. The car pitched deeper.

Daisy's legs were soaked. Her throat was raw. The edges of her palms stung from where her fists smacked at the windows.

The officer looked back.

Where Daisy had earlier thought she'd caught the periphery of a long, straight nose, the hint of a dark mustache, now there was a blank space, like a white sackcloth, tugged tight around soft stuffing.

A doll. A mannequin. A dummy.

The head swiveled on the thing's neck until it was completely backward, its hat tilted to the side, as if it were about to tumble off into the water pooling at his belly. That laughter came again. The sackcloth trembled, as if something inside was moving around, trying to get out.

She thought of the tale of the witches in the woods. Of the supposed curse, made by the man driving a truck, its bed packed with soil and earthworms.

But then: *Curses aren't real, are they?*

Freezing water had reached Daisy's chest. Swirling currents shifted the dummy's boneless form as they pulled the car deeper. "The rear windshield!" Daisy shouted. "Kick it out!" Clark and Maxine turned around, pushed their backs against the wire mesh. "On my count," she said. "Three. Two. One." Their sneakers struck the glass with enough force to make spiderweb cracks. In this position, the water lapped their collarbones. "Again!" Daisy yelled. "Three! Two! One!"

Smash!

The windshield shattered. Bits of glass rained upon them. Daisy reached forward, grabbing the window's edge. They dragged themselves up and out, tumbling to the beach, splashing onto their backs, the ground solid beneath them. A wild rushing sound came from the car as water and air churned. In seconds, it was gone. Down, down, down.

A woman was standing over them, shouting, panicked and angry, wringing her hands. *"What are you kids doing?!"*

Daisy recognized her. She'd been at the desk behind the partition in the police station's lobby. How had the woman gotten all the way out *here*?

Looking around, Daisy saw that she and Maxine and Clark were lying on a patch of concrete. Each was soaking wet, but the beach was no longer there. Neither was the reservoir. Nor the flashing lights, the car, the *dummy*. Instead, they were at the police station's entry. The glass doors were cracked where they'd kicked them.

Daisy scrambled to her feet, took in her surroundings. The quiet street. The nearly empty parking lot. The orange glow of the streetlights. The thick haze in the air. On the other side of the road, just past where the light could reach, she saw a glint of metal—three bikes in the grass.

The woman flinched. "Clark, is that you?"

"Mrs. French," Clark said, flinging his arms around her.

She looked shocked, confused, but she patted his back and then led him indoors. "You're freezing." Looking to the girls, she frowned. "What's this about?"

Inside the entry, the metal stand clutched a poster-board sign reading HOW MAY I BE OF SERVICE? Next to it stood a mannequin, six feet tall, arms and legs stiff, dressed in the uniform of the local police force.

Daisy's lungs fought for breath as she stared into its blank white face. She noticed a series of small tears in the fabric several inches above a square-shaped jawline. From within, a kind of dark cotton stuffing appeared to be puffing outward—a wide, wicked grin.

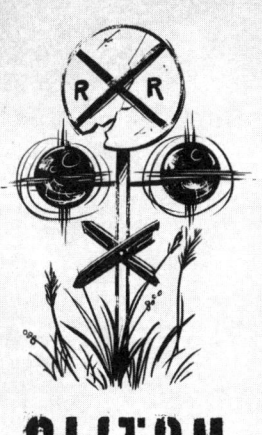

GLITCH

W**hen** the car's radio blared static, Hailey Beckett woke up in the passenger seat of her mother's car. Feeling sick, she unlatched the safety belt, swung open the door, and vomited onto the asphalt. What came out was thin and yellow, tasted like bile and chemicals. She wiped dribble from her chin, then sat back in the seat with a groan. She sipped from her water bottle, swirling a mouthful between her teeth before spitting that out too.

Red lights flashed. The air seemed to shudder. It took Hailey a moment to understand where she was.

Ahead, the CSX guardrail blocked the road. The red *X* of the railroad sign blinked its warning into darkness. Beyond, a freight train moved slowly and steadily along the rails. *Skip-skip-skip-THUD. Skip-skip-skip-THUD.* Some cars were stacked with shipping containers, tagged with bright and expressive graffiti. Others were great white cylinders.

These were marked with decals that read DANGER—FLAMMABLE. Occasionally, an empty flatbed passed, giving her a glimpse of the deserted road on the other side.

Hailey's whole body ached, and the noise of the train thundered in her brain. This wasn't unusual after a trip to the clinic.

Today's visit had been treatment number three. The pediatric unit was brightly colored and filled with books and games, but that didn't make being there any easier. The nurses, Curt and Donna and Purnima, were kind enough, and they always found a way to make Hailey laugh despite her fear of needles. Sometimes her little sister, Evie, would keep her company, and during the infusion, they'd play storytelling, but today, the treatment had been scheduled to finish past Evie's bedtime.

The train went on and on. Sometimes, if you got stuck at the crossing, you had to wait five whole minutes. Maybe more. Hailey had no clue how long it had been, since she'd been napping.

Next week, Hailey would go back for a PET scan, and she *hoped, hoped, hoped* for good news. She and Evie were excited for a potential dance party with the nurses. Hailey had shown Evie how to tape their favorite songs off the radio, and so far, they'd captured Debbie Gibson, Cyndi Lauper, and Michael Jackson.

There was no music playing now. That awful static

continued from the speakers. Hailey clicked it off. It was odd that her mother hadn't said anything when Hailey'd puked, hadn't offered a napkin or the water bottle or even a worried *Everything all right, honey?* Mom sat behind the wheel, her head positioned slightly downward, her hand reaching for the radio as if she were contemplating turning the thing back on.

"You okay?" Hailey asked, her throat aching.

Her mother didn't respond. Hailey leaned forward. Her mom's eyes were half-closed, as if she'd frozen mid-blink. Outside, the train continued to rumble. *Skip-skip-skip-THUD.* "Mom . . . what are you doing?"

No movement. No answer.

Hailey wanted to get home, to take the nausea pills, and then crash onto her mattress. "Mom!" she said, annoyed, then poked at her mother's shoulder.

A shock flung Hailey backward. She nearly slipped off the seat into the road. Her hand stung. Her teeth felt numb. Her scalp tingled.

Confused, she stared at her mother. Something was wrong. The best way Hailey could think about it was Mom looked like some sort of paper cutout. When the cutout flickered, like a TV screen during a thunderstorm, Hailey scrambled out of the car and into the night.

This isn't a joke. It's a dream. A weird one, caused by the chemo.

The train traveled on and on. Behind the partition, red lights blinked and blinked and blinked.

Dizzy, Hailey held the car's hood as she made her way to the driver's side. She opened the door, and her mother flickered again. Hailey faltered backward, then crouched to catch herself. Her meds felt more important now than ever. Their pharmacy usually filled the prescriptions ahead of time and then shipped them to her home.

She *had* to cross these tracks.

The world seemed to teeter as the train continued. Staring at the coming cars, she recognized graffiti that had passed by earlier, painted in the exact same way, as if the railcars were repeating . . . Was she still sleepy? Caught in the remnants of a dream? Here came another white cylinder. Moments later, an empty flatbed rode by. Hailey counted the cars. When she reached two hundred, she gave up. Whatever was going on, it must be connected to her mother's . . . *glitching*. She leaned forward and said, "We're going to be fine. I'll find us some help." It was like something her mom might say if their situations were reversed, and it made her feel better.

Hailey walked down the hill, toward the shopping center. Powerful lamps cast a silver haze. The air wasn't cold, but it also wasn't warm. Strange for late spring. There was no breeze. The sky, which was normally overstuffed with stars, appeared to be entirely black, and yet this didn't look like cloud cover.

Ahead, the stoplights in front of the Price Chopper appeared to be frozen, unchanging. When she reached the parking lot, Hailey noticed how quiet the town was. No cars on the road. No other pedestrians. The glow from the market's sign spilled red and blue onto the pavement, and fluorescent lights revealed aisles of food within. A few vehicles were scattered throughout the spaces closest to the entrance.

Standing near the trunk of a small hatchback, a woman was clutching a grocery bag to her chest. "Hello?" Hailey ran over, but the woman didn't acknowledge her. In fact, she didn't move. Not an inch.

After a moment, Hailey realized the woman's pose resembled the way her mother had been stuck behind the wheel, like a life-size paper cutout. The woman's silhouette flickered. Settled. Inside the store, a few shoppers were also standing still, caught reaching for items on the shelves. Some were tall. Some were toddler size. Each of them flickered. Settled. Flickered again.

Hailey's head hurt and her legs were wobbly. When her knees hit the asphalt, pebbles embedded in her palms.

"Hey!"

Someone was calling from across the lot. A hand extended from the open window of a black pickup truck. Waved furiously. The truck's engine idled. The passenger door swung open, and a stout woman, dressed in denim overalls and a red flannel button-up, rushed to where Hailey had fallen.

"Mrs. Cooper?" Hailey asked, recognizing the substitute teacher's short gray haircut.

"Are you all right?" Mrs. Cooper led her toward the truck.

"What's going on?"

"We're not sure."

We who?

Mrs. Cooper helped Hailey into the truck's cab. A boy in the driver's seat wore a black polo with a Price Chopper name tag pinned to his chest. *Thomas*. She remembered him from shopping with her parents. He always had some joke about whatever product he was scanning at the checkout. A few dark whiskers poked out from his round chin. His long, greasy hair was slicked in a messy side part.

Mrs. Cooper climbed in behind Hailey and pulled the door shut. "Thanks for *the help*, Thomas."

"I didn't want to leave the truck alone."

Mrs. Cooper let out a gruff groan. "This is Hailey. She's a student at the middle school where I teach."

"You get hurt out there?" he asked.

Hailey shook her head. "Something happened to my mom. She's in our car up at the railroad crossing. She's like . . ." She pointed to the woman near the small hatchback. "*That*. We were driving home from—" Hailey stopped herself. She didn't feel like getting into where she'd spent the afternoon. "She was driving. And I'd fallen asleep. And when I woke up, something was wrong. Can you help us?"

"I'm not sure we can do anything." Thomas nodded at the market. "The store is filled with folks acting the same way." He twitched—an unfortunate imitation of the afflicted people.

"It makes no sense," said Mrs. Cooper quietly, almost to herself. "I woke up from a nap on the couch and found my husband... *frozen*... in his lounge chair. We'd been watching *Wheel of Fortune*, but the TV screen had gone static. I asked him to change the channel, but he wouldn't answer me. When I tried to shake him awake, I got this... *shock*. I wanted to call the police, but the phone screeched this awful whining noise. I was walking to the station when Thomas shouted from his truck. Told me what he'd seen."

"I was supposed to work the night shift," Thomas explained. "When I woke up after dark, the clocks in my house were all screwy. I thought I was late, so I rushed over to find... well, *this*."

Hailey's stomach gurgled. She should not have stuck herself in the middle seat. "How do we fix it?"

Thomas stared at the woman by the hatchback. "Probably should figure out what's wrong before we can come up with a solution."

Hailey sank into the leather seat. "It feels like... a dream."

"It does indeed," Mrs. Cooper agreed.

"Maybe it *is*," said Thomas.

They all cracked reluctant smiles.

But then Thomas went on. "We were all sleeping when it happened. Right?"

Hailey nodded. "Would *this* be your dream or mine?" She tried a wider grin, like she might be joking, even though she wasn't.

"Maybe it belongs to all of us," said Thomas, wiping at his nose, his expression now serious.

"You're saying . . . we're all *still* asleep." Mrs. Cooper wasn't having it. "And that we've found one another, *in our minds*?"

Hailey looked around. At the parking lot. At the people. Though she'd only just asked the question, she was already certain that *if* this was a dream, it belonged to her. She couldn't say that aloud; no one wants to be told they might exist only inside someone else's head.

Thomas rested an arm on the steering wheel, looking more sure of his strange theory. "It could be like . . . a story. Like, when you open a novel and read what the author wrote, you're seeing what someone else imagined." His eyes were big, filled with wonder. "Maybe . . . it's like we're all reading the same book. At the same time."

Hailey got nauseous again, but she squeezed her eyes shut and forced the feeling back down.

"You're not making sense," Mrs. Cooper spat.

"And this is?" Thomas raised his hands up to indicate *everything*.

To humor him, Hailey asked, "If this *is* like a story in a book, who's the author?"

Thomas tsked his tongue, held up a finger. "That's what we need to figure out."

Evie popped into Hailey's mind. When she was about three, Evie developed the habit of hopping a few quick steps, stopping, turning, then hopping in the opposite direction. Over and over again. And if you interrupted her, she'd shout, *Leave me alone! I'm daydreaming!* And if you dared ask what she was daydreaming about, Evie would refuse to answer, other than *I don't know!* Evie was five now, and she still did this daily. Hailey wondered suddenly what *daydreaming* actually meant to her sister. She thought of the wild and weird stories Evie would invent while they sat together in the infusion center. She imagined Evie hopping, back and forth, back and forth, coming up with a tale about a world where reality had broken, where a few lost souls had been left behind. Then, Hailey realized: If Evie had been asleep whenever this glitch-thing had *taken over*, then maybe she was awake now. A lost soul too. Alone and scared as heck.

Thomas's eyes lit. "*Or!*" he said, licking his lips. "Or, this is simply evidence that we've all been living in some sort of computer simulation. And the computer's glitched out."

"What if we drive," Mrs. Cooper interrupted. "See if we can reach somewhere that feels . . . normal. Alert the authorities. Get our families some help."

"You can head off wherever you like," Hailey answered, tiredness making her tongue sharp, "but I need to get home." *Before I puke. Or pass out. So I can help poor Evie.* "I don't think . . ." She fought back another bout of nausea. "I don't think I can do it without your help."

"I'll drive you," said Thomas. "We'll check on your family. Then, if you want, or need to, you can come with us. Where do you live?"

Hailey sighed. "That's the thing. My house is across the tracks. And the train doesn't look like it's stopping anytime soon."

Thomas parked the truck in the lane opposite Hailey's mom's car. The train was still going along at its slow and steady pace—*skip-skip-skip-THUD*—maybe twenty miles per hour.

In the road, Hailey approached the driver's door. Her mother was still there. Frozen. Hailey kept her distance. "Mama, we're gonna figure this out. Everything will be all right." Her mother still gave no response, but at least she didn't flicker this time.

Mrs. Cooper watched the endless railcars passing by, her jaw slack, lips parted in awe. Thomas came around the front of his truck. "It doesn't stop."

"I told you," Hailey whispered.

"It's like . . . our record is skipping."

A shared dream. A computer simulation. Here was a new one: a skipping record! Hailey thought of the stereo in her mom's car. The tape deck sometimes ate cassettes, and when you tried to pull them out, the black ribbon inside would snag and unspool. In Hailey's opinion, this was more like that—the world they'd found themselves in was like a section of unspooled tape.

"It's much too dangerous to cross," said Mrs. Cooper, placing her hand on Hailey's shoulder.

"Maybe that's the point . . ." Hailey ducked low and peered beneath the bellies of the rushing railcars. There was more road, a glimmer of streetlight, and illuminated windows in houses just up the street. One of them was hers. "If it feels impossible, then maybe *that's* what we should do." Thomas sniffed. Amused. It made her mad. "What if someone has made this happen? Or something?" Was she the one making weird theories now? "Like . . . the author of that storybook you mentioned. What if the answer is on the other side? The way to stop all of this? And . . . and *the author* doesn't want us to find it?"

Mrs. Cooper shook her head. "I won't watch you fall under these wheels. Not for such a silly reason. There's no author. We're not part of a storybook. Or simulation. Or dream! I say we turn around—"

"The answer *is* over there," Thomas interrupted. "I can feel it. Can't you?"

Mrs. Cooper threw her hands in the air. She paced down

the hill a few steps in a show of refusal. "What about we look for an underpass?" she asked. "An overpass?"

"I grew up walking along these tracks," said Thomas. "The nearest trestle is at least fifteen miles south."

On these twisting roads, it could be at least an hour's trip down and back. Hailey thought of her mom, sitting behind the wheel of her car. Frozen. Glitched. She worried the same had happened to her dad. And worse: that Evie was awake and alone. Finally, she thought of her medicine, which she needed *NOW*, not in an hour, not after a thirty-mile drive. "Earlier, I counted the cars," she managed. "They repeat. If I can get up onto one of the flatbeds, I can jump down the other side."

Thomas scrunched his brow. "That's actually not a bad idea."

He moved his truck parallel to the rails, edging as close as possible to the advancing cars. He lowered the tailgate and then helped Hailey into the cargo bed. She winced as she stood. "You good?" he asked.

"I'm fine," Hailey answered, stretching through the pain. Down the road, Mrs. Cooper stood on the double yellow line, arms crossed, watching them. Hailey caught a glimpse of her mother in the driver's seat, door still open. She inhaled the weirdly stale air and then swiveled herself onto the truck's roof. It was nearly level with the base of the railcars.

"You kids be careful!" Mrs. Cooper shouted, but she didn't make a move to help.

One of the white cylinders passed by. If Hailey's count was correct, a flatbed would be coming along shortly.

And there it was. Rushing more quickly than Hailey had expected.

"Ready?" asked Thomas.

"*No*," said Hailey. She screamed as she jumped, landing on the flat surface of the moving bed, rolling several times.

She spat out some saliva. Checking for injuries, she discovered nothing worse than anything else that had already happened to her. Looking up, she saw that Thomas was still standing on top of the pickup, growing smaller as the train carried them apart. She forced herself onto her knees, then crawled to the far side of the flatbed, where she sat and dangled her legs over the edge. Below, the pebble-filled shoulder was a spotty blur. Hailey didn't hesitate. She swung out her feet, pushed herself away, and then dropped.

Pain erupted from her knee, her arm, her shoulder. When she settled into the dust, she stared up at the railcars passing indifferently into the darkness. Her pants were torn. So was her sweatshirt. Spots of blood bloomed. She forced herself to stand, to put one foot in front of the other, and make her way back to the crossing.

Near the flashers, she peered beneath the railcars. Thomas's truck was gone. Even though he was an odd duck, it would have been nice to have him with her, but Mrs. Cooper must have convinced him to do things her way instead.

By the time Hailey reached her street, the earth was tilting. Dizzy, she knelt on the lawn in front of the Steins' place. Down the block, her neighbors' windows were illuminated by the blue glow of televisions.

Ahead, home appeared. She wanted to run, shouting for her father and her sister. But the darkness inside her house made her think twice. Theirs was the only one on the street that didn't have some kind of light coming from within. Thomas's conversation about *the author* crawled up from her memory, and she thought about how whoever might be doing this hadn't wanted her to cross those tracks. To make it back here. Were these shadows meant to frighten her away?

Now that she was alone again, it was easier to believe this was all a dream, that she was asleep in the front seat of her mother's car, that they were about to pull onto this very block, where Mom's soft touch would tenderly lift her back to consciousness. She hobbled along the driveway, crossed the lawn, crept up the front steps. She flung the door open. "Dad! Evie! Are you here?" She listened, her heartbeat ticking inside her skull.

No answer.

A good sign?

Or a bad one?

Her mouth felt as dry as rocks. She flicked on the light in the front hall. At the kitchen sink, she turned the knob, ducked her head toward the water, gulped down several mouthfuls. They cooled her belly.

A noise came from upstairs.

Skip-skip-skip-THUD. Skip-skip-skip-THUD.

This was what it sounded like when her little sister was *daydreaming*—a race, back and forth, punctuated by hops and turns.

Funny how it also sounded like the train clacking along the tracks.

Skip-skip-skip-THUD.

The ceiling trembled. Drinking glasses rattled in the cabinets. This was right above her. Hailey wasn't alone. Evie was here. Maybe Dad too. Together, they could go back and rescue Mom.

They could find the author... make them stop telling this story... Hailey imagined shouting, *What were you thinking? Treating your characters like this!* She thought of the scans that had first shown her cancer. The tumor that had grown in her abdomen, a bright blue lump against the white background of the light box on the wall. She would shout at the author, *How could you be so cruel?*

Hailey took the stairs as quickly as her tired legs would allow, which happened to be not very quickly at all. At the top, she clutched at the railing, nearly dragged herself onto the landing.

Evie's bedroom door was closed. Hailey tried the handle, but it was locked. The brass felt like ice against her palm. The sound of her sister's *daydreaming* came from inside—*skip-skip-skip-THUD*—the force of it vibrating the floorboards. Hailey pounded on the door with both palms. "Evie! It's Hailey. I'm home!"

The skipping stopped. Heavy footfalls came deliberately across the room. The lock clicked. The door swung inward.

A small silhouette stood in the entry, stared up at Hailey, the head tilted curiously.

Hailey's cheeks burned. Sweat dripped into her eyes. She struggled to see through the darkness. The silhouette shivered, shimmered, its edges all strange. "Evie? Are you okay?" Hailey asked, reaching for her sister's hand.

But the thing that answered was not her sister.

GILBERT KEEPS GOING

The cassette player clicked in his hand, jerking Gilbert out of his reverie. The auto-reverse function had kicked in again. He opened the Walkman, removed the cassette, then dug through the leather satchel. That last one had left him shaky, but not enough to want to stop. Finding the tape labeled *Two*, he slid it from its case, then shoved it into the device. Before he could hit PLAY, he noticed more writing on the wall across the car.

NO EM 'S OO

No em's oo? What did it mean?

From where he sat, Gilbert could see some additional drawings surrounding the new letters. A Ferris wheel on fire. A cop without a face. A railroad crossing sign. All from the stories he'd just listened to. The other riders in the car had not created these. Not the elderly white woman in a paisley headkerchief who looked lost inside her mind. Not the middle-aged

Black man in a gray suit, engrossed in his phone. Nor the aloof young Asian man in a green letterman's jacket.

Gilbert checked the time, but his phone's display was glitching. Lines crossed the screen, turning his wallpaper image of Haku from *Spirited Away* into what looked like some sort of puzzle that needed to be put back together. The clock numbers made no sense. 29:74. They switched. 77:11. And again. 89:42. He pulled up Percy's profile for a new text, but all that came from his typing was garbled nonsense.

He looked to the other people in the car. "Are your phones working?" No one looked at him. "Anyone have the time?" Again, no response. In the city, it wasn't unusual for folks to ignore you or pretend they couldn't hear. Gilbert approached the man in the suit. "Excuse me. But can you . . ." The man wouldn't look up. His response felt too eerily similar to the story Gilbert had just heard. And while he knew that this man couldn't be glitching, couldn't shock him—*right?*—he stepped back.

The train was speeding along. As weird as these other people were acting, he took comfort in not being alone. He'd arrive at his home station sometime within the next half hour, which might be enough time to listen to one more tale. Then he'd consult with Percy about some way the tapes—this new *key*—might help Ant.

Sitting down across from the drawings and the letters—*no em's oo*—he adjusted the headphones and then, once again, pressed PLAY.

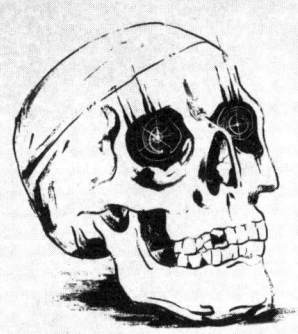

IMOGEN'S SKELETON

"**S**peak up, Imogen," said Mrs. Chung.

The entire class turned to look at her. Imogen's skin prickled. Her face was instantly ablaze. She dug at some gray stuff that was stuck underneath her fingernails. "*I don't know the answer*," she said, louder this time. Mrs. Chung fixed her gaze on the girl for a few seconds before querying someone else.

Imogen didn't know the answer because she hadn't heard the question. She'd spent the past fifteen minutes considering the life-size anatomy model skeleton hanging beside her. Today, its chipped tooth had caught her eye—a detail she'd never noticed before.

Kids at Imogen's school had nicknamed the skeleton Sally. Imogen's desk was in the rear row, in the corner. She could reach out and hold Sally's hand whenever she wanted. Imogen had never done so, but she *could* have.

She ran her tongue across her own front teeth, feeling the

jagged edge where she'd recently cracked her right incisor. (Best not to ask how. You probably wouldn't get the truth, not from Imogen, anyway.) Something else she'd noticed was a small fissure in the skeleton's right radius bone—the exact spot where Imogen had fractured her arm the year before. (The official story had been that she'd slipped in the bathtub.) Recently, depending on the weather, Imogen's arm twinged with pain despite the doctor's insistence that she'd recovered. (This was frustrating because, in Imogen's opinion, which she kept to herself, only she'd know when she was recovered.) Imogen always figured the model was made of plastic, but now she wasn't sure. Why would its makers have built in these flaws? The chipped tooth. The crack in the arm. The color of the bones was yellowish, as if covered in shellac. Hanging from a brushed-nickel frame, they were attached to one another by hooks and screws, and in some spots, some rubbery material that was supposed to look like cartilage.

Could it be that the bones were authentic? Might they have come from someone who'd walked and talked and breathed? How sad to be stuck here, at the back of a classroom in a middle school in the center of a busy city. Possibilities flittered through Imogen's mind: Sally had been a murder victim, or Sally had been kidnapped by an evil corporation who turned kids into models, or Sally had been sick and wanted her remains to be donated to science. If the skeleton *was* real, it felt wrong to let her hang.

"Miss Blankenship!" Mrs. Chung focused on Imogen. Imogen swiveled in her seat, faced forward, as she'd been reminded time and again. "The least I ask is that when I'm speaking, you pay attention. Understood?"

"Yes, Mrs. Chung," Imogen whispered.

Mrs. Chung cupped her hand by her ear. "I'm sorry, what was that?"

Imogen cleared her throat. It was nearly impossible for her to answer the teacher at an acceptable level. When she repeated, "*Yes, Mrs. Chung*," she felt like she was screaming.

While trying to dribble a basketball in gym class, Imogen nearly tripped over her own feet.

"Nerd!" Deanna Loomis yelled from across the court.

Imogen glanced at the PE teacher, Mr. Perlman, who'd pretended to not hear the insult. She tossed the ball to her closest classmate, a boy named Ned, who'd been totally unprepared. It bounced off his shoulder and went loping out of bounds.

"What is *wrong* with you?" Deanna said, scooping up the ball and readying her next move.

Embarrassed, Imogen asked Mr. Perlman if she could get some water. At the fountain, she kept her head low, her long ash-blond hair hiding her red face. Thinking of Deanna, a series of insults whirled in Imogen's brain. For some reason, an image of Sally appeared too, hanging by the tip of her skull from the framework at the rear of the darkened classroom.

Right then, Imogen decided to rescue the bones.

After the last bell, she knocked on Mrs. Chung's door. The teacher was cleaning up, getting ready to leave. Imogen stepped inside, holding a strip of masking tape discreetly in her palm.

"What is it, Imogen?"

Near the desk at the back of the room, Sally dangled helplessly in the shadows.

Positioning herself in front of the doorknob, Imogen said, "I wanted to apologize for earlier." Behind her back, she slipped the tape quickly over the latch, pressing hard so the device stayed inside the door.

"Oh." Mrs. Chung softened. "That's okay. I only need to be sure no one is missing out on my lovely lessons, is all."

"See you tomorrow, then." Imogen was so pleased with herself, she sounded almost happy.

"Don't forget to read the assignment."

Slipping out into the hall, Imogen bolted for the bathroom, where she hid in a stall until the building settled into quiet.

When she was sure she was alone, she crept back to the classroom. Mrs. Chung had turned out the lights, but daylight filtered in through the large windows that overlooked the neighborhood. Through the crisscrossed innards of the security glass, she saw Sally waiting for her. She tugged the knob. Thankfully, her trick worked, and the locked door swung open. Imogen pulled the tape away from the latch and dropped it into the waste bin.

Approaching the skeleton, Imogen couldn't help but smile—something she hadn't liked to do ever since the incident with her tooth. Sally grinned back. Imogen dragged her chair closer to the model's framework. She unscrewed the bolt at the top of the skull. Sally collapsed to the floor. Imogen looked to the door, her heart in her throat. After several long seconds, she figured no one had heard. She cradled the skull. "I've got you," she said softly.

The classroom's windows were hinged at the bottom, latched at the top. Imogen opened one. Lifting Sally from the floor, she eased the skeleton through the gap.

"Wait for me," Imogen said before letting go. The skeleton dropped out of sight.

Imogen passed the guard, who was still stationed at the front door. "Running behind?"

"I had to use the restroom," Imogen lied.

Embarrassed, the guard said nothing as Imogen slunk out of the school.

In the alleyway around back were several large dumpsters. She found Sally lying beside one of them. When Imogen turned the skeleton over, she saw one of Sally's front teeth was missing—the one next to the damaged incisor. Now there was a gap in her smile, as well as a chip. "I'm so sorry!" Imogen whispered. "We'll get that fixed." She cradled the skeleton in her arms, and then made her way back to the sidewalk.

Passersby had all kinds of reactions: horror, amusement, curiosity, worry. Imogen focused on the path ahead. She'd known people would stare, but this was *extra*. Home was fewer than ten blocks away, but she understood that if anyone from school recognized her—*or Sally!*—there would be trouble. She veered into the park where there were hiding places if she needed one.

At her building, the Graylock Apartments, Imogen knew she'd encounter her biggest challenge yet. The doorman, Mr. Phillips. Imogen straightened her spine, made her face look neutral, as if nothing out of the ordinary was happening. (It was something she'd gotten good at over the past few years. Don't ask why. You probably don't want to know.)

Coming up the walkway, Imogen watched Mr. Phillips rush from his station to open the glass doors for her. "What've we got here?" he asked.

"A present for Mom," said Imogen with a wink. She could turn on the charm when she absolutely had to. "Very *hush-hush*, if you know what I mean." It felt like something her brother, Stefan, might say.

Mr. Phillips held a finger to his lips. "Secret's safe with me, kiddo."

"There," Imogen whispered to Sally as the elevator doors slid shut with a ding. She pushed the button for the penthouse. "We're safe now." This wasn't all the way true—being at home hadn't felt safe for quite some time.

Upstairs, she took the service entry and made her way into the hall outside the kitchen. From there, she snuck the skeleton into her bedroom. There was space at the back of her closet.

"Imogen?" her mother called out from across the apartment. "Is that you?"

Imogen peered into the hallway. "Yup!"

Mom appeared in the doorway to the dining room. "I didn't hear you come in."

"Sorry?"

"Stefan's coming home this evening. Just wanted to let you know."

Imogen's skin went numb. "In the middle of the week? What about school?"

"Oh, you know. There was a little disagreement or something. He's taking some time off."

A little disagreement or something... Which meant Stefan had gotten into another fight. How long was the suspension this time? The question made Imogen nauseous. Wasn't the point of boarding school that you actually *stayed* there?

Stefan was only a couple years older than her, but they were polar opposites. Where Imogen thought herself quiet and imaginative and frequently nervous, it was as if Stefan were made entirely of ground meat, his brain included.

"We're all going out to dinner," said Mom, dragging a finger along the hutch where Dad stored his record collection. She flicked away dust. "I was thinking Cheryl's Kitchen. So, get started on your homework ASAP."

Imogen fumed at her desk, scanning the chapter Mrs. Chung had assigned. It wasn't that she didn't want to go out to dinner—she loved the chicken at Cheryl's—but it felt like her parents were rewarding Stefan for behaving badly. She didn't understand them.

She didn't understand *anything*.

She thought of Sally, crouched in her closet.

Imogen got up and cracked the door so Sally didn't have to stay in the dark. Later, she'd figure out what to do with her. Fix her tooth. Find a better spot where Sally could just . . . *be*.

At dinner Stefan refused to speak. He barely looked at anyone. That wasn't the painful part. It was that Mom and Dad were all smiles and chatter, as if everything were hunky-dory. Why couldn't they say what was really on their minds? That they were disappointed in him. Yet again.

Didn't they want things to change? To get better? Didn't they understand what they'd have to *do* in order for that to happen?

On the walk back to the apartment, Stefan crept up behind

Imogen and kicked at her heel. Her foot went flying forward, and she nearly ended up on the sidewalk in a split. Of course, he was almost on the curb by the time Mom and Dad looked back. Dad asked, "Honestly, Imogen, do you think you can try making it *one block* without falling?"

Stefan chuckled to himself.

Imogen didn't let her guard down for the rest of the night.

After she was in her pajamas and the others had settled into bed, Imogen pulled Sally out of the closet. She arranged the skeleton on the mattress beside herself. They shared the pillow. Two skulls side by side. Imogen knew this was strange, but she didn't care. Stefan could apparently do whatever he wanted, and no one said a word. So why couldn't she?

Turning off the lamp, Imogen whispered, "I got you, Sally."

Imogen dreamed of mosquito bites.

She opened her eyes, her whole body tingling, as if numb. Someone was sitting on the bed beside her, compact and pale. Big black eyes stared down. Her first thought was *How did Stefan unlock my door?*

But then her vision adjusted.

When she realized it was Sally on the edge of the mattress, bony fingers clutching Imogen's hand, Imogen understood that this was still a dream. *That* was why Imogen couldn't cry out. Couldn't pull herself away. Groggy, she remembered the term *sleep paralysis* from a television documentary she'd watched with her parents.

The tingling sensation moved up her arm, past her elbow, encompassed her shoulder, crept farther. This numbness was disconcerting. She couldn't even grunt out her annoyance! *Stupid nightmare...*

Ambient light of the night city glowed through her windows. Where Sally had been bone only moments ago, now there was cartilage, blue veins pulsing, whitish nerves spidering across twitching red muscle—new flesh climbing up the skeleton's arm, filling it in. From the edge of her vision, Imogen was horrified to see the skin on her arm was gone.

She understood: Somehow, Sally was taking her.

Bit by bit.

Imogen watched Sally's hand become whole—white skin appearing like an elastic costume as it stretched toward the pinkish shoulder. She struggled to scream, to yank herself away. *Awake!*

Sally's new skin suit was now at her neck. Muscle and veins and nerves spread across skeletal torso. Imogen's own body continued to melt away—everything but her bones.

Soon, her own face stared down from Sally's skull, which was now sprouting ash-blond hair. Two orbs appeared in the sockets, blue irises shining out as Imogen's vision went dim.

And then black.

When she woke, there was a kind of light shimmering from overhead, which Imogen *sensed* rather than *saw*. She could feel her body, upright and chilled, in the corner of a familiar room. Rows of desks stretched before her, a chalkboard on the wall.

Mrs. Chung had just come in through the doorway, tossed her bag onto her chair, placed a coffee mug on top of her desk calendar, leaving another tan-colored ring. The woman ran her hand through her hair, let out a sigh, then shook her arms and jumped up and down several times.

Imogen wasn't able to call out. Nor did the teacher seem to notice her at the back of the room. *Speak up, Imogen*, she heard in her memory. She couldn't move her jaw. Couldn't move her limbs. Couldn't move *at all*. Panic rushed in. She tried to slow her breathing but then realized she couldn't feel breath in her lungs. She searched for the sensation of a pulse. Nothing. She tried to blink. Turn her head. Couldn't do those things either. (Here's something you should know: It's a horrible sensation when you need to scream but cannot.)

Faintly, she sensed the first bell. Slowly, her classmates filtered in through the door. There was awful Deanna, who'd made fun of her during gym class. And sweet Emma, who had always looked at her kindly, but never spoke a word. More and more kids filled the room, leaning toward each other, teasing, gossiping, pushing the boundaries of what they knew Mrs. Chung would put up with before the second bell marked the start of the period. Why was everyone ignoring her? They *usually* ignored her, but this type of ignoring felt new—it was as if they couldn't even *see* her.

Then, Imogen watched *herself* come through the doorway. Strangely, a few of her classmates appeared surprised to see her too. Or maybe they were surprised at how Imogen had transformed from yesterday. This *other* Imogen looked like Imogen, only . . . different. She wore clothes from Imogen's own closet—black jeans, a cream-colored button-down blouse with puffy shoulders and cuffs, white Keds, scuffed soles. But her ash-blond hair was combed in a slick part and tucked behind her ears. And there was something about her eyes. Brighter blue than before.

"I can't believe she's *here*," Deanna whispered to a boy sitting beside her. They were glaring at the other Imogen, who seemed to be pointedly ignoring them. "I heard there was an accident at her place last night. Something about her older brother. Something bad happened to him. A neighbor called my mom this morning. Supposedly, there were police and everything."

What did she mean?

What happened to Stefan? Much of the previous day came up as a blank. *Why couldn't she remember?*

"Well, apparently, *Imogen* is fine," said the boy as he opened his textbook, uninterested in Deanna's drama.

The girl (this *other* Imogen) came down the aisle toward the last empty desk. Imogen (the one we've known) watched as the *other* Imogen moved with a swagger that she had never possessed. The *other* Imogen slid herself into the seat Imogen usually took. Frantic, Imogen could only stare at the back of the new girl's head.

The second bell rang, and Mrs. Chung closed the classroom door. "I hope you all managed to do the reading last night," she said with a smile. "Because . . . I've got a little surprise for you." She removed a stack of papers from her desk drawer. "A quiz!"

The class groaned. Imogen would've killed to be able to take a quiz right now. It would've meant everything was good. A-okay. Ordinary. This was like a bad dream—in fact, Imogen couldn't be sure that it *wasn't*.

As her classmates passed back the quiz pages, Imogen felt someone take her hand. The *other* Imogen was looking up at her with those cold blue eyes. Her smiling lips parted to reveal a wide gap in her teeth. There was the chip that Imogen knew would be there, but then she saw that the adjacent front tooth was missing entirely.

Memories came like a storm, fast as a lightning flash, with a shock just as great. How she'd stayed behind after school. Had dropped Sally out the window. Had carried her home, hidden her in the closet. She remembered dinner with her parents and Stefan. The walk home when her brother had kicked her, tried to make her fall down. Again. Then afterward . . .

Lying with Sally in bed. The numbness. The theft.

Sally smiled wider, then pulled Imogen's hand close to her chest. From this angle, Imogen could see her own bare bones, her carpals, her metacarpals, and her talon-like phalanges. Fingertips attached by metal hooks. If Imogen's heart had remained where it should have been, it would have pounded and pounded to beat this devil.

"Don't worry," Sally whispered up to her, new eyes twinkling like stars—like those glistening swimmers that showed up whenever she'd hit her head, chipped her tooth, broken her arm. The gap in Sally's teeth spread out like a doorway, filling her vision with infinite dark. Imogen worried she might tumble—

Down,

Down,

Down—

And disappear.

The classroom was gone now. Only a voice remained—the one that used to belong to her. It said, "*I got you.*"

BLUEBEARD'S PIZZA

It was well known in one corner of the city that Jake Vaughan's pizza was the best around. People called him Bluebeard because of his long blue whiskers. Some said he used a special dye made from the ink sacs of a rare sea snail. Others were convinced that the odd color grew in naturally. Vaughan had the reputation of being a type of wizard—not a *real* wizard, mind you, but the kind of magical person you might find in the city's peculiar shadows and glittering spaces. His wizardry occurred mostly in his shop on Fifth Avenue—a hole-in-the-wall brick-oven pizza joint that he'd aptly named Bluebeard's Pizza. It had been there for decades, and if you found your mouth watering for a slice, you'd best be prepared to wait in line.

When Mikey Torres's father told him to stop in at Bluebeard's and ask "the wizard" about a part-time job, Mikey was confused. Apparently, Ruben Torres and Jake Vaughan were buddies from way back. But the men couldn't have been more different. Ruben was a clean-cut entertainment lawyer, while Vaughan rarely dressed in anything other than a stained white tank top, Hawaiian-themed board shorts—even in the dead of winter—and faded tattoos that told cartoon stories on his leather-like skin. Imagine Mikey's shock when he learned that, decades ago, the two had played in an indie punk band called Tentacle Rot. ("Don't mispronounce it," Ruben warned Mikey with a grin. "We were the freaks all the mamas warned kids to stay away from.") Vaughan was guitar and vocals. Ruben had been on beats. Mikey had a hard time imagining his ordinary father slamming the skin off a drum kit at the back of a smoky bar, midnight after midnight, in the dim years before Mikey had been born.

He went in on a Tuesday afternoon, when the pizza place was sleepy. The shop was tiny. The oven against the back wall took up most of the space. Pizza boxes were stacked as high as the ceiling. The smell of sauce and cheese and dough was enough to make Mikey dizzy with hunger.

Bluebeard was wiping down the glass counter. His shaved head reflected fluorescent lighting. When he finally glanced up, it wasn't to say *hello* or *how can I help you?*—it was simply to stare and wait, as if the burden of speech was solely on whoever dared walk through his door.

Mikey wasn't surprised. He'd gotten plenty of pizza from Bluebeard's. This was how it usually went. Except, *today* wasn't about getting a slice. He kept it simple. "My dad said to talk to you."

"Who's your dad?" The man's gaze was a growl.

"Ruben Torres. You and him are buddies from way back?"

Attitude peeled away from Bluebeard like tires on asphalt. His wild grin showed graying teeth. *"Ru-ubes."* He drew out the nickname as if it were a song lyric, then let out a rough laugh. "Where's he been at?" Mikey didn't have a chance to answer. Bluebeard stomped emphatically. "Tell that loser he better stop in before I make it my business to go find him."

Mikey quivered. "I will . . . do that."

"Ruben told you to come talk to me? What the heck for?"

A bunch of words bounced around in Mikey's head. *Bike. Job. Part-time. Tentacle Rot.* He reached for the most important ones: "I want a bike."

"You want *a bike*."

Mikey went rigid. "I need a job so I can get a bike. Or, really, so I can pay my dad back for the bike he got me already."

"Better be a nice bike." Bluebeard considered him for a moment, then showed those teeth again. "I can give Ruben's kid a job. Sure. What are you good at?"

"I . . . like pizza?"

"Not really a skill." Bluebeard shrugged, then whacked at the counter with the damp rag. "Come back tomorrow. We'll figure you out."

Mikey started the next day in the back room, folding boxes, pressing the premade creases, tucking flaps, stacking them one on top of the next. Juan and Bob worked beside him, doing prep work—chopping veggies, slicing meat, pureeing tomatoes and herbs, spinning dough high in the air. Linnea, who was only a few years older than Mikey, managed the phone out front. From where he sat, he heard her long fingernails—*CLicK-ClacK-Click-CLIck-CLackETY-ClaCK*—on the register's keys.

Mikey's stool was beside the huge refrigerator. Beyond, in a tight corridor, were three doors. One opened onto a cramped toilet. Another led to an alley. The third door remained locked, with a tattered paper sign that read: ABANDON ALL HOPE, YE WHO ENTER HERE . . . IN OTHER WORDS . . . KEEP THE HELL OUT. Bluebeard had signed it with three little hearts, as if it were a jokey love note.

ClicK. Clack. CLIck.

Mikey glanced up. These sounds hadn't come from Linnea at the front of the shop. They'd come from the corridor. Curious, Mikey peered into the dark space. The noises came again. He checked the bathroom. Empty. No one was in the alley either. Despite the sign on the other door, he tried the knob, but it wouldn't budge.

Click. Click. Click.

"Hello?" Mikey pressed his ear to the metal. Was someone asking to be let out? "You hear that?" he asked Juan and Bob, who were busy at their stations. Neither seemed concerned; if it weren't for Bluebeard's warning to keep out, Mikey probably wouldn't have been concerned either.

After his shift was over, Linnea snagged his shirtsleeve before he could head out. "You don't wanna get paid?" she asked playfully.

"Oh, right," Mikey said, his mind elsewhere.

She opened the register, used her acrylic claws to dig out a couple twenties. "Juan and Bob told me you were asking about that door in the back. The one with the sign."

Mikey blushed even further. "I was just curious."

"Killed the cat!" said Linnea.

"I didn't . . . kill anything."

"I was talking about *curiosity*, doofus. But listen, stay away from there. I know he seems like a softy, but Bluebeard is touchy about it."

Months passed, and Mikey slowly paid back the money his father had lent him. A few times a week, he'd ride his bike to the shop after school, and when he was done, he'd scoot on home, up the hill to the brownstone where he lived with his dad. He liked the crew—Juan, Bob, Linnea. And Bluebeard was like a rock star, bursting into the joint with fresh ingredients, turning heads with his unique look and raspy voice. Once, Mikey examined some of these odd veggies and herbs in the fridge. Certainly they hadn't come from a local grocery. They had spikes and barbs and fuzz. When he asked Bluebeard about them, the man answered, "Professional secret." This only made Mikey more curious about the locked door at the back of the shop.

One night after work and dinner and an hour or so of TV, Mikey was getting ready for bed when he realized his gold chain was gone. The necklace had been a gift from his mom before she left. He searched his bedroom, the kitchen, even the bathroom, but the chain was nowhere to be found. Had he dropped it at the pizza shop?

Surely, Dad wouldn't let him head back there this late, so Mikey snuck out with his bike.

Except for the blue neon glow of the sign in the window, the front of the store was dark. He cupped his hands at the glass to block the glare from the street. A light was on in the back room. Mikey knocked, but no one answered.

In the alley behind the buildings, he leaned his bike by the door. To his surprise, the knob turned in his hand. A moment later, Mikey found himself in that tight corridor.

Though the lights were on, the work space was empty. The refrigerator's motor hummed. The pile of boxes he'd spent the afternoon constructing was nearly depleted.

Beneath his stool, he saw a glint of gold. The chain's clasp must have come undone. He quickly pocketed it. But before he could head back outside, he noticed the forbidden door—the one with the sign about abandoning all hope—was slightly ajar.

At the bottom of a skinny flight of stairs was a spare basement room, the brick walls painted white, like the work space at the back of the pizza shop. The gray concrete floor was spotless—as clean as the countertop where Linnea spent afternoons slinging slices. Her earlier words came to him: *Stay away from there . . . Bluebeard is touchy about it.*

Even so, he couldn't keep himself from heading down.

The sight of a dilapidated maple cabinet stopped him short. It stood about six feet tall, three feet across. At the front, two doors mirrored each another. Their centers were decorated with small circular medallions and oblong sunburst carvings. A tarnished key stuck out of a hole, a red ribbon tied to a loop on its end.

The air felt strange down here—as if he were pushing through a pool of crystals that caressed his body as he moved. He pulled at the red ribbon. Both doors creaked. When he caught a glimpse of what was inside, he blinked.

A long hallway reached out, darkness waiting at its end. Many closed doors marked either side. Red velvet wallpaper. A wood-paneled ceiling. A plush runner rug with intricate Persian designs caught pools of amber from gaslight sconces.

Mikey stepped aside, peered around the back of the cabinet. There was a gap between it and the wall. He shuddered. *Is this some kind of Narnia situation? Or maybe a dream?* Instinct told him to walk back up the stairs and ride away.

But curiosity is a type of enchantment, and Mikey found himself suddenly under its spell.

In the cabinet, a flickering appeared in his peripheral vision. Embedded in the wallpaper were pulsating gossamer threads. He had a sudden idea of what he'd stumbled upon. There were stories about secret nightclubs scattered around the city. *Speakeasies*. In a working laundromat, you might find a hidden door disguised as a stack of washing machines that led to an arcade. Or in a Chinese restaurant, a mirrored panel would open into a popular dance club that operated only at night. *This* was why the door at the top of the stairs had been locked during the day, and why the alleyway entry had been unlatched.

Bluebeard's secret was that he had a business *beyond* pizza.

Feeling confident, Mikey called, "Is anyone here?" Farther down the hall, one of the doors creaked open and someone stepped out. This person wasn't the wiry man with the weird beard he'd been expecting, but a woman, dressed in a cobwebby gray gown and long black gloves. Alabaster antlers rose up from a headdress, draped with gauze that hid her face. She placed one hand daintily on the wall as she stared at him. Growing up in the city, Mikey had encountered strange fashions, but this costume might have been the strangest. He felt his cheeks flush. "Sorry to bother you," he said. "I'm looking for . . . a friend." The woman's antlers crooked as she contemplated him.

There was another creak as another of the doors opened. Then another. And another. Several figures entered the hallway. None of them looked human. One wore a frock made of feathers, a rainbow explosion that burst outward from a ruby-red sternum. Hair sparked from pale skin at the edges of a face, whipped up into a wide purple halo, bright yellow eyes like a cat's or snake's. Another was dressed in a black-tailed tuxedo, but their skin—their entire body, head, hands, and whatever was hidden by the clothing—appeared to be made of giant colorless fish eggs, all clumped together, their gloss reflecting the lamplight.

Mikey's throat started to close. He understood that these weren't costumes and this was no nightclub.

Abandon all hope, ye who enter . . .

A firm grip clamped his shoulder. Mikey screamed as he tumbled backward into the fluorescent light of the pizza shop's basement.

Bluebeard stood over him, wearing a look of shock and anger and . . . *fear*? He slammed the cabinet shut and turned the key with the red ribbon. Inside, a latch clicked, and something about the air shifted yet again. Bluebeard's breath was heavy, his fists wound up tight, veins pulsing on his tattooed skin. "What are you doing down here?"

"I lost my chain," Mikey managed, flipping out his pocket. "I saw the light on in the back room. I thought . . . I thought . . ."

Bluebeard huffed, then held out his hand. Mikey worried

that if he took it, the man might crush him. "Get up," he said. Mikey pushed himself off the ground. When they reached the workroom upstairs, Bluebeard locked the door behind them.

Mikey could only stare sheepishly at his sneakers. Images from inside the wooden cabinet blinked in his mind. His body twitched, his shoulders jerked, his head cranked automatically atop his neck as if it were trying to jump off and run away. He wasn't sure if this was from his tumble out of the wooden cabinet, from seeing the red hallway, or if something in his brain had gone kablooey.

Had he seen what he'd thought he'd seen?

Had those things been . . . *real*?

Bluebeard pointed to a stool. "Sit. I've got to explain something to you. And afterward, I need a promise."

Only then did Mikey truly understand that he might walk away from all of this with his bones, and life, intact.

"There are places in this city that glimmer," Bluebeard said. "And there are places in this city that gloom. Further, there are some places, few and far, that do both. You've just encountered one of them. Hear me?"

Mikey heard, but he had no clue what it meant. "How does something . . . *gloom*?"

Bluebeard explained in the only way he could—by telling a story.

Long ago, a powerful magician called November had a bad falling-out with his sister, a woman named October. The reason they'd broken was that November sought a kind of wisdom not to be found in the world they'd known, and October believed he was overstepping boundaries. There were books, *forbidden*, that he wished to add to his collection, filled with remedies and recipes and spells.

Unable to reconcile, November ventured far from their small town to the mouth of the nearby river, in search of an entity, a kind of sentient black hole known as THE VOID, that he'd heard could eat holes in the very fabric of reality.

When November located THE VOID, he offered a deal. Using the doorways that THE VOID created, November would travel to eldritch places, these magical *Elsewheres*, to locate the tomes of which he'd heard rumor, and in return, November would use his new magical knowledge to protect THE VOID from those who would exploit and harm it. You see, some folk feared these doors, feared the beings that existed in those beyond-places. There were some who would have rather THE VOID not hold the power that it did.

So, THE VOID agreed.

November gained his knowledge and even shared some of it with his sister, hoping to restore her trust.

The doors to *Elsewhere* remained open. However, in the process, certain *Elsewhere* beings found their way through to our world. Keeping his promise to THE VOID, November used his new mastery to create little realms of safety for these beings—pocket universes where the *Elsewhere* travelers might hide. The wooden cabinet in the basement was such a pocket, where they could come and go as they pleased. November asked men and women whom he trusted to act as guardians of these realms.

Over time, the guardianships passed from one generation to the next. Bluebeard inherited a cabinet from a family member. At night, he'd leave the door unlocked, so the beings could come and go. This was the very cabinet in the shop's basement.

The one Mikey had climbed into.

Listening to the tale, he felt dizzy. "You let those monsters out into the city?"

"They're *not* monsters," Bluebeard replied, his face weary, as if he'd had to convince many others.

"Then what are they?"

"My dude, they're *people*. Like you and me. And just like people, some of them are kind. Some can be cruel, but there are rules in place to keep us all in check."

"A sign on a door in the back hall of your pizza joint?" Mikey wouldn't have dared say it, but his head was hurting now, and he maybe wasn't thinking the way he once might have.

"It's worked. Until *you* came along." Bluebeard's eyes became slits. "Remember when I said you had to make a promise?" Mikey nodded. "You're gonna tell no one what you've seen. There are bad folk in this city who would literally *kill* for what's in that basement." He cleared his throat and crossed his arms. "If you weren't Ruben's kid, I'm not sure we'd even be *having* this conversation. I would've just closed the doors on you and locked them. Understand what I'm saying?"

If the man was trying to scare him, it was working. "Yes," Mikey answered.

He rode home up the center of the street, glancing every which way in case some *glimmer* or *gloom* had decided to follow in the shadows.

Back in his bedroom, Mikey set the broken chain onto his dresser. He was too freaked out to switch off the light or even get under his covers. He lay, corpse-like, and stared at cracks in the ceiling, considering what his boss had shared, what he'd seen, how the residents of the cabinet had all looked eager to come for him, to protect themselves . . .

Or maybe, they'd been hungry.

CLicK-ClacK-Click-CLIck-CLackETY-ClaCK.

Mikey shot up out of sleep, body clenched as he scanned his room frantically for the source of the sound. Someone had turned off his bedside lamp. Now the streetlight was trying to peek through the closed blinds. In the sudden silence, he crept to the window, hoping a bird or a branch had caused the tapping at the glass. But nothing was outside.

Click. Click. Click.

This time, it came from behind him.

A silhouette appeared in the mirror over his dresser, but it was not his own. In the dimness, he made out the face of his co-worker Linnea. Her long acrylic nails scratched impossibly from the other side of the mirror glass. "Mikey, we're in danger," she whispered.

Mikey wished he were more surprised to see her. He leaned closer. "What kind of danger?" he asked, thinking of the *glimmers* and *glooms* Bluebeard had mentioned earlier. And then, "How are you doing this?"

"We don't have time," she said. "Take my hands." She tapped her nails again. *Click. Clickety. Click.* "Pull me through."

Through the mirror? "I don't understand."

"You opened the door!" she answered, a desperate whisper. "The people of the cabinet are angry. They're coming."

So, she knew too!

He pressed his hands against the glass. Linnea's fingers clamped onto his own. Her fingernails dug at his skin.

"Now pull!" Linnea begged.

Mikey threw his weight backward, but Linnea didn't budge. A glimmer of a smile appeared at her lips.

Suddenly, he understood.

She hadn't needed help. She'd only wanted to catch him, hold him there. A spider and her fly.

"What is this?" His voice shook.

"*You opened the door*," she said again. "My people are angry."

Mikey tried to yank himself away, but Linnea gripped his forearms and pulled him closer. No smile now. Instead, a spark lit in her eyes. "*Your* people?" he choked out.

"I told you to stay away from there. But maybe I lied about Bluebeard. He's not the touchy one. *I* am."

Mikey wanted to scream for his father, but he knew that wouldn't turn out well for either of them. "I won't tell anyone. I promise!"

"You've put us all at risk. A promise from you doesn't count for crap, *doofus*. I'm gonna need more than that now."

"I'll never come back to the shop. You'll never see me again."

"Oh, yes I will. Every day, you'll come back. But you'll be working for *me*."

"For you? Doing what?" Mikey hoped she meant running the cash register and answering phones, but deep down, he knew she didn't.

"A little of this. Little of that. Take care of things need taking care of." The look on her face told him that these were not the types of errands *anyone* would want to do. "You'll come every day. You'll work your shift. And then later, we'll work *together*."

Mikey yanked back hard from the mirror, but her fingernails, *real* claws now, tore at his skin. He held in a shriek, blurted out, "Bluebeard said that there are rules. To keep you all in check."

"You of all people, mentioning rules? Ha. What are these rules, Mikey? Do you know? Will they keep us from coming for your dad? When he sees our faces in the dark, will he call us monsters like you did earlier this evening?"

I'll tell Bluebeard anyway, he thought. *He's a guardian. He won't let you do this.*

Mikey might as well have said this last part out loud. "Try it," she dared. Before he could stop himself, Mikey thought, *I just might.*

Linnea dragged him closer, so his forehead was pressed against the mirror glass. Her pale face was so angry, it seemed almost to glow. Small slits appeared across her skin, like hundreds of tiny paper cuts. To Mikey's horror, the slits opened, revealing little bits of onyx tucked inside. Within each, golden embers smoldered.

It was clear now, the path forward, like a red hallway leading into shadow.

"You just might, eh?" Linnea echoed, clutching him more tightly. The embers in her skin grew brighter, illuminating her side of the mirror like dawn fighting through the blinds. "In that case, I'll have to keep my eyes on you."

THE BUREAU OF BLACK HOLES AND SUPERNOVAS

December is darkness. November is what's coming. October is the magic that prepares you for the other two.

A girl named January Bowen said this to me the summer I turned twelve. We met in a writing class in the city, at a secret workshop called the Bureau of Black Holes and Supernovas, located in an unassuming storefront on Fifth Avenue, across from one of the best pizza joints in the neighborhood.

The Bureau's exterior was made to look like a place where you'd get your taxes done. Inside, metal shelves lined beige walls. They were stuffed with white cartons and boxes labeled UNCANNY SYRUP and PORTAL POWDER and GLITCH REMOVER and STARDUST and THAT FUNNY FEELING YOU GET SOMETIMES LATE AT NIGHT. Framed posters hung on the walls—images of galaxies and clouds of space gas and satellites circling planets in unknown solar systems, of shattering suns, and pits of gravity so deep it was difficult to tear away your gaze. Phrases printed at their bottoms read: *Strive to Become Nothingness. Better to Explode Than Fade Away. Always Orbit Before You Land. In THIS Universe, We Believe Stories Matter.* And, *What Can One Say About THE VOID That Hasn't Already Not Been Said?*

Against one wall of the long, skinny room sat a single desk, behind which was stationed someone who always wore a dark suit with black sunglasses, hair slicked back, and a grim expression. A single red telephone rested on the desk. I suppose you could have purchased any of the shelved items from this person. But their true purpose was to act as guardian of what was known fondly as *the gate*. When you signed up for a class, you got a password that you'd tell the guardian. They would lift the red phone's receiver, and the closest set of shelves would swing inward—a hidden doorway that led to the *actual* Bureau of Black Holes and Supernovas.

In a secret back space, an expansive studio looked out over a cloistered garden behind neighboring brownstones. Here were desks and tables stacked with books and papers and cups stuffed with pens and pencils and crayons and scissors. Here, the walls were painted with murals that made you think of science fiction movies from the sixties and seventies. Here were boxy silver consoles that looked like they had some important purpose in the navigation of flying saucers.

Here were other kids, as curious as I ever was.

The studio was founded a decade earlier by a renowned and subversive novelist. Its writing workshops for kids were what had made it famous, and also the whole point of the place. When I was young, I wished to be a storyteller. For most workshops, you could just stop in at the Bureau and sign up. But the class I wanted to take, How to Scare Yourself, was their most popular, and there was a months-long waiting list. The teachers were volunteers—local writers whose curricula changed with the seasons. By the time my number came up, the man who greeted my group introduced himself as Mr. Poblocki. He was tall and broad, with a bushy brown beard that turned red in certain light and eyebrows so blond they looked almost invisible. His voice was expressive and musical, with a hint of rasp.

I'd heard of him, read some of his books, even. Creepy stories for kids. A good match for us.

One of the first things he mentioned was that "stories are doorways to other worlds." I'm sure he wasn't the first to come up with the idea, and others have probably said it better, but it struck me then as important, as if, by wanting to share my thoughts and ideas, I might contain a rare kind of power. I wrote the quote on my notepad, as did the twelve other kids who'd given their passwords at the desk out front on that Saturday morning.

Recently, I found my old notepad and rediscovered the

names of my classmates, which I'd scrawled in the margins. Carolyn, Keira, Alicia, Jerrod, Katie, Paul, Barbara, Maggie, Nana, Stacey, Ramdasha, and, of course . . . *January Bowen.*

She sat beside me at a small table near the windows. When I first saw her, I thought I was dreaming. (Not really, but *almost.*) She wore a raggedy brown dress, shiny silver stockings that went up over her knees, a cluster of brightly colored ribbons tied at her wrists, black boots that were caked with dried mud. Her dark hair was long and curly, fairly greasy, and it was tied up on top of her head with another ribbon—this one acid green. As I squinted, I noticed blue markings on her neck. Drawings maybe? Her style made her look like she'd come from another planet. And after hearing her speak, I remember thinking this might actually be true. As Mr. Poblocki tried to settle us, she turned to me and said, "December is darkness. November is what's coming. October is the magic that prepares you for the other two."

I asked her what that was supposed to mean. She tilted her own notebook so I could see the quote at the top of the page. I shook my head, confused. "Just a little something I wrote about my family," she told me. "Something that struck me as *true.*"

"Your family?" I echoed.

"They're . . . *odd*, you might say. October is my aunt's name. November is my uncle. I'm the daughter of December. The Bowens. We mostly live up north. They say I'm the baby of the family. Occasionally, people call us witches. Most of the time, I let them."

"Are you?"

"Am I what?"

"A witch?" Her boasting didn't impress me. Growing up in the city, I'd met plenty of self-proclaimed pagans, Wiccans, and other practitioners of esoteric arts. Nearby, there were magical stores that catered to all sorts.

January smiled and shrugged. "I'm visiting November at his apartment in Aldridge Place for the summer. He pulled some strings to get me into this class."

That made me light up. "You like scary stories."

"That's why we're here, isn't it?" She laughed. Wide-mouthed and clumsy and swooping and silly. "But I *do* like them," she said. "I could tell you some doozies."

I tried to be kind. "By the end of the summer, hopefully, you'll be able to share them with the class."

"Mmm." She squinted at me, looking almost annoyed that I hadn't begged her to tell me the stories *RIGHT THEN*. "Hopefully."

Mr. Poblocki clapped his hands. "Let's begin!"

We started with a discussion of what made stories scary—of why we were drawn to them, despite the discomfort they might cause. The class came up with many answers, but the one I liked the most was the one Mr. Poblocki finished with: *Battling stories that scare us makes us brave.*

He had us do writing exercises. We brainstormed elements of story: setting, character, action. He told us to draw the creepiest ghost we could think of and, next, to give them a name, a history, a place to live, and most important, a want, a desire, a wish.

I couldn't.

I remember feeling as if my brain were glitching, as if I were no longer capable of dreaming up ideas. Strange. My parents always teased me that my imagination was almost *too big*.

Briefly, I blamed the girl next to me, thinking she was a distraction. Or maybe—just maybe—I worried January really *was* a witch. Not like the ones I knew from around the city. A different kind. And she'd stopped my thoughts before they could form, just to spite me.

We spent time listing our fears, reading them aloud. There were a few that felt typical: clowns, sharks, serial killers, aliens, monsters.

Then some of the students mentioned things I'd never imagined to be frightening—loneliness, family secrets, breaking the rules, being lied to, visiting somewhere new, getting lost, getting found out.

It was these that made our teacher's face glimmer with excitement. "Go deeper. Think about what feels just out of reach. Then grab for that."

Our assignment for the next week was to think of our

story elements, and use those to develop the opening lines of a tale. "Think of the first line like a hook," our teacher said. "One so sharp, it will snag the reader and drag them along, whether they want to follow or not."

The next Saturday, I returned with nothing. I mean, I forced myself to complete the assignment, but I didn't feel comfortable sharing what I'd written. Strangely, the others were in the same predicament. Our teacher seemed baffled, frustrated, as if he were the one who'd failed and not us. We did more exercises he hoped would get us back on track. Word associations. Memory games. Asking the question *What if?*

During a break, when Mr. Poblocki had stepped out front to speak with some other volunteers, January stood before us. "I can help you," she said.

"But I want to do this myself," said one of the students.

"Oh, you'll do it yourself," said January. "All I'm saying is ... maybe there's a reason none of you were able to come up with an idea that made you happy." She raised an eyebrow, as if to suggest—proudly—that *she* was the reason. Her mention of her witch family came to me, and I almost started laughing. She glared. "Do you want my help? Or would you rather waste your time?" The way she spoke kept us quiet for a good long moment. I sensed the fear in the room. Finally, we agreed. What could it hurt? "Pay attention to your dreams this week," she said with a wink. "I bet you'll find them inspiring."

I recall how, for the next few nights, in bed, a dream

version of January appeared like a guide. Together, we'd step into a wooden cabinet where a dark hallway was lined with countless doorways. One by one, January opened them and showed me what was inside. The images are dim now: bleak and foggy seascapes, nursery rhyme music that sounded almost familiar but not quite, smoke that glimmered and gleamed, open graves that roiled with massive red worms, birthday gifts that shuddered and shook, an entity who was like a walking, talking black hole, whose name was sucked away from my brain as soon as he spoke it aloud.

And tentacles.

So many tentacles.

The next time we met, the class was excited by our opening sentences. They were atmospheric and heartfelt and creepy as heck. When we read them aloud, Mr. Poblocki's smile nearly cracked his face open. We spent that day developing those ideas. January didn't say a word about what she might or might not have done to help. In my mind, it seemed entirely plausible that she'd visited us in our dreams. At our little table, I whispered to her, "Thank you." She shrugged and kept writing.

By the end of that session, Mr. Poblocki was so pleased, he made a proposal. "If you can whip these into shape, I'll put them on tape for posterity. I have a local radio contact who might air them a few at a time this coming Halloween season."

We gasped and hollered and whooped. It was the kick in the pants we needed. When we returned to the Bureau the next week with finished drafts, Mr. Poblocki suggested some revisions. Then we helped him record the stories onto tapes. I loved hearing what everyone had come up with. Tales of cursed seashells. Of abandoned amusement parks. Of cemeteries that won't let you leave. Of grown-ups gone mad. Of dolls who feed on the energy of children. Of a bestiary book whose creatures can be coaxed to life.

I felt like I was part of something bigger than myself—like each of us, our stories hidden within, was strong alone, but together, we added up to something more.

In the last few moments of that class, January Bowen began to laugh. A few of us pulled her aside, and she told us a new story. Something about how her uncle, November, had asked her to do this, *to help us*. She recalled what Mr. Poblocki had said about stories being *doorways to other worlds*. That because of some *spell* she'd done, our thirteen tales, when read together, would open a *literal* door, to a *literal* other world. We didn't believe her, of course.

January got angry. "If you don't appreciate me, I can take back my help," she said.

"But the stories are already written," I replied. "They're done."

She blinked slowly, three times, then clicked her tongue. "That's what you think."

Something strange happened that week. I remember nightmares, feeling as if I could not wake, as if every night was an eternity, as if sleep was a kind of gravity I could not escape. These were different than the images January revealed from behind the doors in the dark hallway. Bleaker. Filled with blood and pustules that looked about to pop. Parking garages where bad men locked you in the airless trunks of cars. Hospitals where body parts were collected from the morgue in clear plastic bags. Potluck dinner parties where our grinning neighbors served raw meat in pastel-colored casserole dishes. It got so bad that by Friday night, I was terrified to get in bed.

The next day, Mr. Poblocki had some new project he wanted our class to work on, but we couldn't pay attention. My friends looked as tired as I felt. Our eyes were sunken and dark. Spines sloped. Some of us were jittery. Others, listless.

January looked fine. In fact, she seemed to almost be shining. I dared to play her game. I asked, "Why would your uncle have wanted us to open a door to another world?"

She grabbed my hand, squeezed it emphatically, as if pleased to see that I'd come around. "So he can learn what's inside. There's knowledge out there. Knowledge one cannot discover in this world alone. Do you appreciate what we've done for you?"

I nodded yes, too frightened to give any other answer.

December *is darkness. November is what's coming. October is the magic that prepares you for the other two.*

I hadn't thought of those words, or of the girl called January, in years, decades maybe—the same amount of time since I've tried my hand at fiction. They might have stayed locked away in my mind where, I know now, there exist pocket universes, little places of unreachable imagination.

To my surprise however, I read the quote again this week, as I was going through my daughter's homework. It was marked in her notebook, in her own handwriting.

"What's this?" I asked.

"Something from a story I read at school," Jess told me. "Something that struck me as *true*."

If stories are doorways to other worlds, then memories can sometimes be the keys that open them. In my mind, a lock clicked and it all came back. The Bureau of Black Holes and Supernovas. The red phone on the desk. The guardians with slicked-back hair. The entry to the workshop through the secret portal. The friends I made.

And the girl who'd given me nightmares.

I looked again at my daughter's notebook. "What was the story? Where did you get it?"

"My new friend January shared it in the library, from

a book called *More Tales to Keep You Up at Night*." My skin went tight. "By an author named... *Dan Poblocki*." She looked pleased to recall his name.

I felt like I was going to be sick.

"January said I *had* to read it," Jess went on, tracing her fingers across the marks her pen had made. "These lines are from a story called 'The Bureau of Black Holes and Supernovas.'" She looked up. Smiled at me. "The weird thing is, I'm pretty sure the story was about you, Daddy."

GILBERT GETS A CLUE

A hissing came from the headphones as the train continued apace. The second tape was finished.

Placing the headset on the seat, Gilbert shuddered and then stretched. The other passengers had gotten off, but he couldn't remember the train making any stops. He checked his phone again, but now the screen was black. When he hit the power button, nothing happened. Getting up, he found no passengers in either adjacent car, and the doors were both locked. The train rumbled and shifted, rumbled and shifted, racing along the rails. Gilbert thought of the train from the "Glitch" story, how it had been endless.

Endless.

Other tales whispered in his mind. They were unsettling—some of them downright scary—but the last two had stuck out for a separate reason. They'd mentioned places Gilbert already knew. Bluebeard's Pizza was a few stops from his apartment on the express train. And across the street from that was the writing workshop, the Bureau of Black Holes and Supernovas, famously hidden behind its fantastically bland facade. These had to mean something—evidence maybe that the tales were *more* than just tales?

All the stories shared multiple ingredients. But what did they have to do with Ant? It was like Gilbert was chewing on some new answers, even while the corresponding questions were stuck in the back of his throat.

The writing on the wall across the way caught Gilbert's attention again. Of course, there was more—three additional stories, three additional letters, three additional drawings. Now it said:

NO EMBER'S OO

No ember's oo? His brain made a sudden connection, pieces of the tales from the tapes clicking together like magnets. In the first story, hadn't Tony worked for a company called Ember's Exterminators? But then, another piece from another tale matched up too. In that last one, January had said her father's name was December. Her aunt went by October. And her uncle was November.

It wasn't *"No ember's,"* but *"No-v-ember's."*

November.

Familiar characters. Shared ingredients.

In the tale about the cemetery, the GPS device had been created by a group called November Corp. And in the pizza-shop story, November was a magician.

And then there was their family name. Bowen. Why did that feel familiar too?

On the wall, NOVEMBER'S was apparent, but the OO part was still an unknown. What other letters might change its meaning? Gilbert wasn't sure he wanted to learn. At this point, all he wanted was to get to Percy's house, give them the stupid library book, and try to figure out—

The library book!

He grabbed it from the satchel. Checked the cover.

Elsewhere Gardens.

And the author: October Bowen.

October. November's sister, like January from the "Black Holes" tale had mentioned. Again, in "Bluebeard's Pizza," the titular character had shared November's history. In that story, the siblings hadn't seen eye to eye. October was why November had gone away, left his family behind.

Gilbert turned to the epigraph at the beginning, where October had written, *May these plants find you when you need them most, same as this book.*

What did it all mean?

If October Bowen was a real person, did that mean November was too?

December is darkness. November is what's coming. October is the magic that prepares you for the other two.

If November was a magician, then certainly, so was his sister.

Gilbert's fingers tingled, and for the first time in a long while, he felt less alone. And yet, without a concrete answer, the connections between the tales and the world around him were starting to feel like a web. Sticky. A trap.

Ant's voice message suddenly rang in Gilbert's mind, and his heart pumped faster. He understood now why Ant had sounded so desperate for him to *not* listen. If Ant had heard the stories—and he almost certainly had—then maybe he'd experienced all of this too. And if Tony, from the first tale, had *really* been Ant . . . if Ant *had* encountered that spider-wolf creature . . . or something like it . . . would that happen to Gilbert next?

Stiffly, he perched on the bench.

The answer was simple: He *wouldn't* listen to the final tape.

He'd ride the train until it stopped and then hop off wherever that was. Aboveground, if his phone still didn't work, he'd ask someone for help.

November would not get to him. Gilbert only had to wait it out.

And wait he did . . .

The train rumbled and shifted, rumbled and shifted.

Again. Again. Onward and onward.

After some time, Gilbert eyed the pull brake across the way—the red handle that would grind the car's gears to a halt. He stood, felt the weight of the handle in his palm. The darkness past the windows reached to him, asked him to reconsider. If the train were to stop, he'd have to walk the tracks. What might he encounter along the way? Something with tentacles? Spikes? Fangs?

What if the door January mentioned in that last story was now cracked partially open and Gilbert was stuck in a kind of nether-gap? A place between *Elsewheres*?

In a way, wasn't Ant trapped there too?

He sighed and sat back down.

If stories were doorways, then maybe the only way for either of them to escape was to finish the tapes.

ICE CREAM TRUCK SYNDROME

DAY ONE:

The girls were batting around a badminton birdie in the yard when they first heard the tune—a jangling, happy chime riding on the soft, piney breeze. It made Dagmar think of a nursery rhyme her granny might have once hummed to her before bedtime.

But something about it was off.

The chords went minor when they were supposed to go major. Some notes were held for longer than she expected.

Weirdest of all, Dagmar began to salivate.

"Ice cream?" Victoria Hunter blinked and then shuddered, as if coming out of a daydream. "I don't remember ice cream trucks ever being on the island."

"Me neither," said Cassandra Hunter. Cass was Victoria's sister.

Back home, the three girls swam on the same team. Over the course of several seasons, they'd become good friends. Sleepovers, birthday parties, carpools to competitions in other towns, in other states.

The thing was: The Hunters had money. Dagmar's parents did not.

Since this was the first time they'd ever asked Dagmar to join them on the island, she couldn't say whether a passing ice cream truck was unusual or not. She'd loved riding the ferry, seeing the family's grand clapboard house, having a bedroom all to herself. Being invited here was like stepping through a magic portal and encountering a newfangled version of herself. Victoria and Cass had let her borrow some of their clothes to play tennis at the club. Even her voice was changing as she picked up the cadence of the local kids, whose families had been here for generations, whose tongues might have been coated with tiny, expensive jewels. Worried she might do or say something to upset the balance of the happy trip, she'd kept her opinions to herself.

The jangling tune twisted as it moved into the distance. "I want a Drumstick!" Cass yelled, dropping her badminton racket and dashing around the side of the house toward the street.

"I want a Creamsicle!" Victoria followed, leaving Dagmar holding the birdie.

From the front yard, they all watched a white van-like vehicle disappear around a corner near the beach. "We missed it," Victoria whined, wiping her long brown hair out of her face. With a huff, Cass dragged her fingers through her strawberry blond bob, then tucked it under her cap again. Their mother knelt near the roses at the front steps. "Mom, can we go to Aldridge Place instead?"

Aldridge Place was the ice cream shop in the little town just down the hill, near the ferry dock. Dagmar's mouth watered more just thinking about it.

"Mom?" Cass tried. But Mrs. Hunter kept her back toward the girls, as if she hadn't heard them.

"Earth to Mother!" Victoria bellowed like a brute. *"Ice cream!"* Still, Mrs. Hunter sat lost in thought.

Who knew what went on in the minds of grown-ups?

Cass tapped her mom's shoulder. Mrs. Hunter let out a shriek.

She grappled Cass's forearm, digging her fingers into her daughter's flesh.

Cass screamed, and Victoria yanked her away.

By the street, Dagmar held her breath.

Mrs. Hunter stood. Her yellow floral sundress was spattered with something dark. She held up red-smeared hands. "I'm-m... sor-ry." Her words muddled in her mouth. She looked down at her broken rosebushes. "What... happened?"

Clearly, she'd tried to yank them out of the soil. Curious, Dagmar inched closer.

Cass cried out, "You hurt yourself!"

Victoria picked up the garden hose and switched on the nozzle. Cass directed her mother's hands under the flow, and the red washed away, revealing deep cuts where thorns had sliced their mother's palms. "Oh my goodness," Mrs. Hunter said, coming back to herself. "I ruined my roses," she whispered. Dagmar ran inside to grab a glass of water and some bandages. When she returned, Mrs. Hunter accepted the glass. Victoria tended the wounds. "I'm going to lie down. You girls go get that ice cream."

Minutes later, the three were strolling quietly down the hill, freaked out by what they'd just seen.

"Mom probably just got dehydrated," Victoria suggested.

Cass nodded. "She usually keeps a water bottle within reach. I didn't see it today."

A hot breeze made the pine branches dance overhead, and the dry grass at the edge of the road went *shhh*.

At the Aldridge Place shop, the door was locked, the lights off.

"This stinks!" Victoria grumbled.

Cass cupped her hands at the window, trying to peer inside. "What a waste of time."

When they'd arrived a couple days ago, the little shopping district had been bustling. Now only a few people were out and about. "It was a nice walk at least," Dagmar offered.

Victoria took her hand and squeezed. "I knew there was a reason we brought you with us," she said with a smile.

DAY TWO:

The girls had barely laid out their towels when, down the beach, a trio of tanned teen boys plopped down a bunch of beach bags and chased each other into the waves.

"Who's that?" Cass asked, slathering on sunscreen.

"Never seen 'em before," Victoria said, rolling over on her towel, adjusting her sunglasses, and fluffing her hair.

Bossa nova music played from the girls' boom box.

"Oh wait, isn't that little Nick Turner?" Cass asked.

"Not so little anymore. He'll be a sophomore next year."

"I thought he was in eighth grade, like me."

"He's cute." Dagmar blushed as she realized she'd said the words out loud. The sisters squealed with laughter. Dagmar tossed a bit of sand, and then all three were up, chasing each other, kicking up clouds of dust.

A group of four women who were sitting a few dozen yards away scowled at them. Cass waved and then did a cartwheel. The women scowled harder, wrapping their brightly colored caftans tightly around themselves.

The girls splashed into the surf.

Dagmar's muscles tensed. "Yowza. That's chilly."

"Wimp!" Victoria teased, diving under a breaker. She pointed herself toward the boys and pulled the backstroke. Cass rolled her eyes, then hooked elbows with Dagmar, dragging her against the current. In the distance, the bossa nova station blared. The women in the caftans continued to look annoyed.

Then Dagmar made out a different kind of music. She planted her feet in the sand, and Cass bounced away. It was the tune from the previous day—the song of the ice cream truck. Dagmar thought of Mrs. Hunter and the rosebushes. How she'd spent the rest of the evening unable to use her bandaged hands. How when Mr. Hunter had come home, he'd wanted to take her to the club's infirmary, but she'd insisted she was fine.

Over the tops of the dunes, Dagmar watched a white vehicle passing along the road that circled the outer edge of the island. The tune was that same nursery rhyme—warped, a little off, as before. Her mouth felt funny again. Wet. Slightly salty.

"Hey!" Cass called out from behind her. "That's our stuff!"

Dagmar saw that the scowling women in caftans had approached the girls' beach towels, their umbrella, their bags.

One woman, dressed in sheer white—a hot pink bathing suit peeking out from underneath, auburn curls blowing in the breeze—picked up the boom box from the sand. The bossa nova mixed strangely with the ice cream truck's chimes. The redheaded woman opened her mouth and let out a full-throated *yawp*, then dashed toward the line of surf, carrying the radio over her head. The other women chased as she careened into the water.

"Hey!" Cass yelled again, jumping the breakers.

The red-haired woman reared back and then threw the boom box into the churning white of an approaching wave. The bossa nova cut out. Dagmar gasped. Cass growled. As they emerged onto the sand, the four women faced them. The wind plastered their clothes against their bodies, whipping at the fabric, making them look like ancient statues.

Cass looked ready to explode. Dagmar snatched at her wrist. "Wait," she said, remembering Mrs. Hunter's confusion the previous afternoon.

Footfalls padded from behind them. "What happened?" Victoria asked. She'd brought the three boys with her. Everyone stared at the women.

"She threw my stereo in the water!" Cass yelled.

"Not cool," said one of the boys.

The woman with the red hair was inching forward. Her hands were shaking. Twitching. Her head spasmed atop her neck. Then, the jangling chime was back, the white vehicle passing again on the road behind the dunes. The nursery rhyme tune grew louder.

Two of the other women lunged at each other, falling to the sand, pulling hair, scratching skin. Another dashed into the ocean, swinging her arms wildly, screeching like a seagull as waves knocked her backward. Still, she rose up and ran farther out, yelling louder than before.

The redhead sprinted toward the kids.

The girls screamed. The boys yelped. They took off in different directions.

Dagmar followed Cass and Victoria up the beach toward the dunes.

The white vehicle was already racing away, down the road.

The girls climbed through the tall grass, looking back in wonder and fear. Defeated, the redhead plopped onto the sand, her sunhat flopping over her face. The other two were still fighting, caftans ripped to shreds. And the last woman—the one who'd dashed into the water?

She was gone.

DAY THREE:

At the club, it was lemonade and iced tea all around.

Dagmar sat at a patio table under a black-and-white-striped umbrella with the sisters and the boys from the beach yesterday. It was midday, and the July sun was trying its best to beat them down. Dagmar's tea glass was dripping condensation, a trickle, like the sweat running down the back of her neck. The cabana was nearly empty.

"I heard they haven't found Mrs. Reade yet," said Nick. She was the woman who'd floundered her way out to sea.

"And the others?" asked Victoria. "Her friends?"

"The families are keeping hush. As per usual."

As per usual, thought Dagmar. Tongues coated in jewels.

Today, the girls had accompanied Mr. Hunter while he met up with some friends for a round of golf. They'd run into Nick and his pals Nash and Brad at the cabana cafe. Mrs. Hunter was home. She hadn't been herself since the rosebush incident.

"Does anyone have a clue what made them do it?" This was Nash, all tan and lithe, his eyes hidden behind dark aviators.

Cass and Victoria glanced at each another. Dagmar was surprised none of them had spoken their worries out loud. She was afraid if she mentioned her fear, the others would laugh her all the way back to the ferry.

"I bet it was sunstroke," said Brad, blond and blue eyed, with shoulders that would beg to play football come autumn.

"So freaky," whispered Nick. "I've never seen anyone drown before."

"Let's not jump to conclusions," said Cass. "Mrs. Reade might be all right. Somewhere, safe and sound."

"Right," said Victoria. "Und Affen fliegen aus meinem Hinterteil."

Nash raised an eyebrow. "What's that supposed to mean?"

Cass's lips curled. "Don't ask."

Nick shared rumors that other locals had been acting funny the past few days. Neighbors arguing audibly into the evening. Aggressive posturing at a bar near the docks. Someone had even smashed out the front window of Betty's Island Boutique, around the corner from the ice cream shop down the hill. This news made Dagmar want to call her mom and ask whether coming home early was an option.

Their waiter, an older teen Dagmar hadn't seen before, approached and asked if he might refill drinks, maybe bring some lunch. But before anyone could answer, that now familiar (and nightmarish) chime filled the air.

Dagmar glanced toward the parking lot, where she made out a blur of white passing slowly through the rows of parked cars. She stood and pointed. "There. *That's* what's causing it. The song."

All eyes were on her. Accusatory. As she'd feared. How dare she mention something so ridiculous? That the chiming of an ice cream truck was violently affecting some people who happened to hear it? Cass pulled at Dagmar's elbow, trying to get her to sit. Without thinking, Dagmar pressed her palms to her ears.

Their waiter grunted. The tune from the parking lot grew

louder. The waiter's hands trembled, just like the redheaded woman's at the beach the previous afternoon. His head knocked toward his left shoulder before whipping rapidly toward the right. Then he swiped at the table, shattering the drinks onto the ground.

The group pushed back from the table, but the waiter managed to snag the collar of Nash's polo shirt. He tossed the boy aside before lunging at Victoria. Dagmar dragged her friend out of reach. Everyone raced away from the waiter, knocking patio furniture over to block the path.

It worked. The older teen toppled to the ground, hit his head against the pavement, and stopped moving.

Cass clasped at the sides of her ball cap. "Is he . . ."

"Who cares?" Nick yelled. "He just attacked us!"

The tune from the white vehicle grew louder still. Dagmar's palms couldn't block it out. Whoever was behind the wheel had come here to . . .

What? Infect as many people with this bizarre syndrome as possible?

From the putting green, there came another commotion. The six kids watched as two elderly men raised their golf clubs toward each other. Before they could swing, Dagmar averted her eyes. This did not keep her from hearing the awful thudding sounds, nor the shouts and cries of her friends who hadn't thought to turn away.

DAY FOUR:

Just after dawn, Dagmar woke with a gasp. At first, she didn't know where she was. A moment later, it came rushing back. They'd spent the night inside the guest cottage at the far end of the Turner property, adjacent to the pool.

Dagmar was curled up on the couch in the den, a fuzzy throw half covering her bare legs. Earlier, Nick had pulled the blinds to keep their location hidden, but now the pale glow of morning was streaming in, casting hazy bars of sunlight across the bamboo floor.

The previous day was like a bad dream. As members of the country club had rushed around the course, the kids huddled inside the clubhouse, peering out through tinted glass, unwilling witnesses to the sparking violence. All the while, that chime jangled from the parking lot like a death knell. A curse. In the aftermath, only a few of the adults outside remained standing—weary, unsure of themselves, unaware of what they'd done.

Even before the white vehicle finally pulled away, taking its song with it, the kids knew they couldn't go back to their families. What if the same was happening to their parents? Their siblings? Instead, they'd snatched golf cart keys from the administration desk. Cass had driven one cart. Nash took another. Together, they'd zipped through back roads to this place, sequestered and safe.

Now the others were still asleep on different sofas. Through the doorway to the bedroom, Nick and Nash had passed out on top of the covers.

Overnight, they'd kept the windows sealed and locked. The air was sticky and hot. Dagmar found it hard to breathe.

In the kitchen, an avocado green telephone hung on the wall beside the small fridge. She lifted the receiver, held it to her ear. The previous afternoon, when they'd arrived, she'd wanted to phone home, to tell her mother what was going on, but the line had emitted a dull busy signal. They hadn't even been able to call the island police. This morning, the phone was silent.

"Any luck?" Cass was standing a few feet away.

Dagmar shook her head. "Dead," she whispered.

Minutes later, the others began to stir.

They showered, trying to make the day feel ordinary. Nick cooked up bacon and eggs, then they sat around the small table in the dining nook. They tuned the radio to the closest mainland station. A stream of pop songs. No news indicated any problems out on the island.

Later, they argued about what to do next. Cass and Victoria wanted to check on their parents. "They've probably worried themselves into a tizzy," said Victoria.

"We've never not come home before," Cass added.

"I don't think it's safe," said Nick.

"Maybe things are back to normal," Brad suggested. "Maybe it was all a fluke."

Dagmar had an idea. "What if we explore? See if anyone needs our help?"

"*We* need help," said Victoria.

"I can make a sign," said Nash. "Post it on the front door."

Nick frowned. "Why don't you just shout out, 'Come get us, zombies'?"

"No such thing," Cass answered with a frown. Dagmar knew she was thinking of her mother.

"We could try for the ferry," said Brad.

But no one wanted to risk going that far.

In the end, they decided the safest move was to stay put, listen to the radio, see if anything changed. They had food enough for a few days and running water and electricity.

Dagmar picked a book from a shelf, something with a romantic cover. Beautiful people embracing. She skimmed page after page, but her mind wouldn't allow her to absorb the story.

In the afternoon, Brad peeked through the blinds, into the yard by the pool. He flinched and immediately drew back.

"What's wrong?" asked Nick.

"Your dad's out there."

"Is he okay?"

Brad shook his head. "I think . . ." He gulped. "I think he saw me."

Nick shoved him aside, looked out the window himself. He shouted, "Everyone get back!" Before he could jump away, the glass shattered. A metal chair careened into the living room.

"Run!" Victoria yelled. Cass and Dagmar followed her to the opposite side of the house. They ran out the back door. Dagmar turned to check on the boys. The three were struggling with a large man she'd never seen before. Cass pulled her around the corner where the golf carts were parked. Victoria had already started the engine. It sputtered as she pressed her foot against the pedal. Cass and Dagmar managed to jump on as the cart sped down the driveway toward the service lane.

"We can't leave them!" Cass shouted.

"And we can't stay here," Victoria said, gunning the motor.

"We're going the wrong way," said Dagmar when Victoria turned onto the main road. "The ferry is *down* the hill."

"I need to check on Mom and Dad."

Dagmar clutched the vinyl seat. Cass bit at her lip.

At the Hunters' place, Victoria steered the cart up over the curb. Dagmar grabbed the side rail to keep from spilling onto the asphalt. Without a word, the sisters sprinted up the front walkway.

They had no plan . . . "Hold on!" Dagmar called out.

Too late—her friends swung the front door wide and then disappeared inside. She felt exposed. Something about the house made her think of the dead phone line—nothing there, no connection. What was left of the rosebushes was scattered across the front lawn. Mrs. Hunter must've finished what she'd started.

Dagmar crept to the hedges that lined the property and hunkered low into the evergreen needles. Keeping her eyes on the front door, she waited.

And waited.

Had an hour gone by? More? Without a wristwatch, Dagmar could only judge passing time by the sun overhead and shadows slanting on the grass.

The front door remained open a crack.

Finally, she approached. "Victoria? Cass?"

From the landing at the top of the stairs, there came a shuffling sound. Then a groaning.

Dagmar backed away. She slid behind the wheel of the golf cart. Started it up. Pulled off the curb. Pointed toward the village, where they should have gone in the first place. She scrubbed at her stinging eyes. Looking back, she pressed the center of the steering wheel, a last-ditch effort. The horn sounded, brief and bold. Instantly, Dagmar knew she'd made a mistake, marking her location for all to see.

There was movement at the front doorway. *Please be one of the girls*, she thought. *Pleeease.*

When a tall figure emerged onto the porch—*not* one of the girls—she understood what had happened to them.

At the ferry dock, Dagmar parked behind the ticket booth. She sat for a few minutes, fighting for breath, pushing bad pictures from her brain.

The map kiosk showed the schedule. The evening ship should already be here, waiting for passengers. Had no one else thought to ferry it the heck out of there? Or had the mainland learned what was going on and decided to stay away?

Just after sunset, Dagmar noticed a shadow creep from the alleyway behind the shops. She tensed, realizing she had nothing to protect herself. She hid at the corner of the ticket booth. As the person passed below a streetlight, she recognized one of the boys. Nash. His face was flushed, his dark hair matted and crusty with what . . . blood?

Was it safe to call out?

When he approached the map kiosk, Dagmar realized that he'd had the same idea she'd had. Which meant . . .

He's okay?

"Nash," she whispered.

He spun. In one hand, he clutched a knife. Trembling, he raised it toward her. She stepped into the light, holding up her own shaky palms. "Dagmar?" His voice was scratchy. No more jewel-coated tongue. "Are you alone?"

She nodded. "You?"

He ran to her. She nearly fell backward. Seeing the panic in her face, he stopped short, looking to his knife. "I'm so sorry," he said, and Dagmar understood. He'd wanted to give her a hug.

She wasn't ready for that. She waved for him to join her on the far side of the ticket booth. "*I'm* sorry. We tried to get Victoria to wait for you all."

"That wouldn't have helped."

They sat, staring at the ocean. The sky was violet, but a smear of orange spread across the horizon.

Neither offered to tell their story of the day.

Clearly, the others hadn't made it.

"The ferry's not coming," Dagmar said.

"We should find somewhere to hide. Somewhere not outside."

Keeping to the shadows, the two crossed back toward the shopping area. A soft sound came from up the hill. Someone wandered aimlessly in the street but didn't notice them.

Nash tried several shop entries. All were locked.

Dagmar spied a boarded-up window. The sign overhead read BETTY'S ISLAND BOUTIQUE. She and Nash padded over, keeping their sights on the person up the hill.

"How do we get in?" Nash asked.

Dagmar tried the door. No luck. Examining the board at the window, she realized it had only been propped into the frame. Carefully, they removed the wood, leaned it against the building, then crawled through the opening, crunching onto broken glass.

Nash sighed, realizing that replacing the board from inside would risk noise. But Dagmar held up a finger. There was another door at the back of the shop.

Beyond, a small hallway led to the building's other business. Aldridge Place Ice Cream. When Dagmar tried the knob and it turned, she almost squeaked with relief. Inside the ice cream parlor, she twisted the lock.

Nash checked the front. Gave a thumbs-up.

They had their camp for the night, safe from the afflicted. But since the storefront was entirely glass, it would be safer to stay in the office.

Stores of sugar cones and ice cream toppings were hardly a meal, but they managed to keep hunger pangs at bay. Dagmar made short work of one bag of mini pretzels, wishing instead for her mother's homemade gazpacho with crunchy round toasts.

To keep their minds off the day, they sat in the dark and spoke about their lives. Turned out, Nash's family didn't have a home on the island either. He'd been coming out to spend summers with Nick for years. Brad was a newer friend. They attended the same private school. Participated in debate club, which Dagmar found surprising. Dagmar shared stories about swimming with the sisters—of Cass's fierce loyalty, of Victoria's penchant for mischief, of how their relay team was one of the best in the state.

As her eyelids began to droop, Nash worked up the courage to change the subject. "What do you think is happening here?"

Strangely, Dagmar hadn't allowed herself to truly consider this, mostly because what was happening didn't seem possible. The simplest answer: "Someone is trying to hurt us?"

"But how?"

"The song. The white truck. It . . . it does something to your mind."

"Not to *our* minds," he answered.

"They're . . . targeting adults. Or at least, people older than us. The waiter at the club—"

"That guy couldn't have been more than seventeen."

"I was thinking sixteen. And he totally flipped out when he heard it. But it didn't work on us."

"Someone's targeting adults *for what reason*?"

Dagmar caught a whiff of debate club. She shrugged. "Maybe we should stuff our ears with wet napkins."

"Maybe." But he didn't make a move.

"It feels like something out of a horror movie."

"Or a nightmare."

"Same thing?" Sitting in the dark, the coolness of the tile floor seeping up through her shorts, she could almost sense Nash's grin. She remembered seeing the boys at the beach for the first time. How her immediate reaction had been: *so cute*. Was it a cliché that this felt like a lifetime ago? "What's the plan?" she asked.

"We get the heck off this island."

"And what if the same thing is happening back home?"

Nash didn't have an answer for that.

DAY FIVE:

Hours later, Dagmar woke up shivering. The refrigeration from the ice cream coolers kept cold air close to the ground, and there hadn't been anything in the shop to use for blankets.

Nash was at the desk chair. A small lamp glowed. He shuffled some papers.

"What are you doing?" Dagmar wiped sleep from her eyes and drool from her mouth.

"You need to see this." Nash handed her a page. A brief letterhead read *November Corp*. The handwritten note below had been dated the week before.

> Dear Mr. Aldridge:
> Per our agreement, you shall fulfill duties beginning Monday. The arrangements have been made. My office is unlocked and waiting for your arrival. There you will find all that you require.
> I shall expect a daily report. Do not disappoint.
> Sincerely,
> N. B.

"What is this?" Dagmar asked.

Nash shook his head, dismissing the question. "During our sailing lessons, me and Nick and Brad would pass an old naval base at the far side of the island. It's all fenced off. There's a lighthouse and some abandoned barracks. One day, we got close enough to read a sign posted along the shore. NO TRESPASSING. And underneath, I'm pretty sure, was printed BY ORDER OF NOVEMBER CORP."

Dagmar let the paper fall from her fingers. "You think . . . that's where—"

"The office. It's got to be where this N. B. person told Mr. Aldridge to go."

"And Mr. Aldridge is the Aldridge of Aldridge Place Ice Cream?"

"I'd assume so. Didn't you say Monday was when all this started? The first time you heard the song?"

"Yeah. And later, when me and Cass and Victoria came down for ice cream, *this* shop was closed."

"Aldridge was already at the office. At the base."

"We need to go there. Now."

The keys jangled in Dagmar's pocket as the two ran toward the dock where she'd left the golf cart. Nash was clutching the knife, glancing around, looking out for any of the *afflicted*.

The streets were quiet. The sky was that pale non-color that comes just before sunrise. Despite the water-soaked napkins they'd shoved into their ear canals, Dagmar could still hear muffled birdsong chattering from inside the dark pines that towered over the shops.

Dagmar drove. Nash was navigator. The cart's top speed was a bit faster than a grown man could run for his life.

By the time they made it to the crackled asphalt that led out to the dunes, the sun was peeking up over the ocean, turning the few clouds at the horizon a bright pink.

Dagmar parked near a busted chain-link gate, upon which a small white sign with simple black lettering had been posted. NOVEMBER CORP. A long, squat building made of blond brick was across a wide parking lot. Beyond, the lighthouse stood, its red and white stripes like a barber's pole. The glass at its peak was dark.

Nash waved for Dagmar's attention, then pointed at a white van parked at the side of the bunker. In the open, there was nowhere to hide, so they raced toward it, fast as they could.

Up close, the van looked like something a kidnapper might drive. A black utility speaker had been bolted to the carriage over the driver's side door. Dagmar wanted to climb up and tear it off, throw it to the pavement, and stomp it till her feet bled.

This was no ice cream truck.

At the partially cracked door, Dagmar was tempted to remove her earplugs, to gauge if there was anyone inside, but she was too scared to risk hearing something she'd regret.

Here was a kind of mudroom. Empty coat hooks. Storage cubbies. A doorway on their right opened onto a long space with a high ceiling. The air was stale with the stink of sweat and a hint of . . . *something nastier*. Morning light poured through the windows facing the water. Furniture was sparse—folding chairs, a couple large plastic bins. Old nautical gear was piled in corners—coils of thin white rope, ring-shaped floats, a few orange life jackets. A wide shelving unit stood directly in the center. Papers were scattered on a nearby table, a box of cassette tapes in its middle, the kind someone might use in a car stereo . . . or a van with a state-of-the-art speaker system. Beside the tapes was a bright red phone, its wire connected to a socket in the wall.

Dagmar almost reached for the receiver, but stopped when she noticed a calendar hanging on the wall. This week's Monday had been circled in red ink. In each of the next four boxes, someone had marked *GEN OMEGA*. In the fifth box, *today's box*, were the words *GEN ALPHA*. She glanced at Nash. He looked as confused as she was.

Just then, someone coughed. Even through their makeshift earplugs, they'd heard it, and they knew they weren't alone. Nash tugged the pointless paper wads out of his ears. Dagmar did the same, then pointed to the bookcase. When

Nash started toward it, she almost yanked at his shirt, but his knife glinted in the sunlight, and she knew they had no other option.

On one of the shelves, Dagmar noticed an odd-looking pistol. A flare gun. She grabbed it. Empty. Still, it looked threatening. Nash held the knife flat against his sternum as he approached. Dagmar's heart galloped. She squeezed the handle of the gun.

Nash peeked around the unit's edge. Swiveled back. Gulped breath. Waved for Dagmar to look.

An elderly man was lying on a cot. Eyes closed. His pink scalp shone through his messy white comb-over. He was dressed in a yellowing tank top and a pair of board shorts. Plastic flip-flops dangled from his bare feet, which hung over the cot's rusting edge. Thick headphones covered his ears.

Nash gestured over his shoulder, mouthing, "Rope."

The old man shifted, snored. Dagmar grabbed a rope coil from a pile of gear.

When she came back, the old man's eyes were open. Nash was pointing the knife at him. Mr. Aldridge sat, raising his hands, afraid. His gaze flicked between them.

"Don't move!" Nash yelled, the knife tip wavering.

Mr. Aldridge nodded, a show of compliance.

"Put your hands behind your back." The man did as he was told. "Dagmar, tie his wrists."

She licked at her lips, the unreality of the situation

settling upon her. Things like this weren't supposed to happen to kids like them. Kids like them didn't do things like this. She tucked the flare gun into the waistband of her shorts. She'd never tied anyone's wrists before—never tied anyone's *anything* before. His elderly skin was papery and thin and moist. Looping the rope around and around, she made a tangle she hoped wouldn't come loose. She gave it several hard yanks, then, to scare the skinny coot, she snatched away his headphones. Mr. Aldridge's body jolted, and he let out a cry. Dagmar took out the flare gun and made herself look ready to use it.

"Who are you?" the man asked.

"*We're* asking the questions," Dagmar heard herself say. "Got it?" Mr. Aldridge nodded. "And you're gonna answer them or . . ." *Or what, Dagmar?* "Or else." The old man stared at her, disbelieving. She felt her face growing warm. She couldn't let him see that she felt like she was about to wet herself. "Who sent you here? Why are you hurting people? How is . . . *all of this* . . . happening?"

Mr. Aldridge's jaw clenched. "I . . . I can't . . ."

Nash steadied the blade. "Answer her."

"If I do, something bad will occur."

"Something *bad*?" Dagmar barked a laugh. "We know you're working for someone. Someone with the initials . . ." *What were the initials again?*

"N. B.," Nash finished.

"Yeah! Who's N. B.?"

Something in Mr. Aldridge seemed to break. He stared at the floor, his eyes glazing over. "I'm sorry. I'm so sorry. None of this was supposed to happen."

"*Who is N. B.?*" Dagmar repeated, louder this time, shaking the empty flare gun at him.

"Mr. November," Mr. Aldridge answered. "I made a promise a long time ago. This was all supposed to be some kind of experiment. The music . . . It comes from . . . *Elsewhere.*"

"*Elsewhere?*" Nash asked.

"November believed it might have an effect on the listeners. He wanted to see what would happen. Something about . . . *control.*"

"Control?" Dagmar echoed. "Like . . . mind control?"

"I was to drive the truck. Play the track. Observe. Report. I did it all, even as things went awry."

"You mean, when the adults started attacking everyone?" Nash spat out. "You observed that. Reported back. And then did it again the next day?"

"Everyone knows you can't break a promise to Mr. November. He wanted to learn about . . ." Aldridge shook his head. "You kids won't understand—"

Dagmar didn't want to hear excuses. "What's Gen Omega? What's Gen Alpha?"

Aldridge blinked slowly. "Generations. There was one tape for the Omegas. The elders. And then, today . . ." Tears smeared down his cheeks. "Today, I was supposed to put in a new tape. For the Alphas."

"For the kids," Dagmar said. "For *us*."

"Our friends are gone," Nash said quietly. "Their families . . ." He couldn't speak the word. "This is your fault."

"Are those the tapes on that table over there?" asked Dagmar. "The Omegas? The Alphas? When were you planning to start? After you had some coffee?"

"You have to let me go. I can't break my—"

"Your promise?" Nash finished. "Yeah, we heard you."

Dagmar ran to the table and dumped out the box of cassettes. Opening the cases, she tugged at the little black ribbons with her fingernails, then ripped them apart. She called out to the man, "I just broke your promise for you!" When he whimpered, she felt a pang of joy.

Her eyes fell again upon the red phone. She lifted the receiver, held it to her ear. She wasn't sure if there'd be a dial tone, a busy signal, or silence.

Turned out, what she heard was none of those things.

It was a voice—low and rich, like a stringed instrument, and as it spoke, she felt a sensation like nothing she'd ever experienced. As if . . . her bones were shivering. "What do you need?" it said.

Dagmar couldn't speak.

"You know I don't like to be kept waiting, Aldridge," said the voice, pronouncing the name differently than Dagmar had been doing. More like ... *Eldritch.* Dagmar let out a breath, and the voice changed, as if suddenly aware of her. "Who ... is ... this?" it asked, deep and dark as an ocean trench.

Dagmar hung up, feeling suddenly drained.

"What did you do?" the old man shrieked from behind the shelving unit. *"What did you dooooo?"* His crying rose into an almost melodic wail that echoed through the space, making Dagmar think of the song he'd spread around the island.

"We have to leave," she whispered. She gathered her strength, planted her feet, then, shoving the voice from the phone out of her skull, she shouted, "Nash! We've got to go!"

Outside, they found an old dinghy overturned beside the building. Its aluminum body had been painted white, an emblem from the old naval base on its bow.

They flipped the boat, pulled it across the bleached pavement and onto the beach, its bottom digging a groove into the sand.

At the water, Nash told Dagmar to wait as he ran back into the depot.

She checked the horizon. Waves were quiet on this side of the island. A breeze carried Mr. Aldridge's screams. *Hurry, Nash,* she thought. *He's coming.* She knew this now. *November is coming for us.*

Relief gushed in her veins when Nash reappeared,

dragging a couple of oars, another rope coiled over his shoulder. He was wearing the headphones she'd snatched off Mr. Aldridge's skull. His pockets bulged with other supplies. "Take these," he said, holding out four flares.

They pushed the dinghy into the surf. Freezing water soaked her legs, splashing her clothes, making her quiver. They climbed in. The boat dipped and rose over the rolling waves.

Nash hauled the oars against the current, steering in a direction Dagmar could not decipher. Facing backward, she noticed that the top of the lighthouse was flashing.

Blink . . .

Blink . . .

Blink . . .

Who . . .

Is . . .

This . . .

She imagined speakers posted somewhere at the naval base, loud enough to cross the water and seep into their heads. She removed the flare gun from her waistband. Slipped one of the ammo cartridges into the chamber. Clicked it shut. Then, with a sorry glance at Nash, she took the headphones.

"We'll switch back and forth," she said. "When you get tired, let me know."

Nash nodded, eyes wide, as if unable to talk. It was just as well—Dagmar placed the phones over her ears and the world went silent. She knew that if any sound were to blast out from the coast, only one of them would be safe from it.

Nash rowed the boat.

And Dagmar clutched the knife.

THE MAN AT THE DOOR

Tommy stopped crying at exactly 3:33 p.m.
Heather knew this because when the house went quiet, she checked the clock on the fireplace mantel. She and her older brother, Clay, had been keeping an eye on Tommy while their mother was running errands. At three and a half, Tommy had recently decided that naps were annoying, especially when his siblings were around; hence the tantrum. Heather was about to go check on him when the doorbell rang.

Clay went to answer it, but Heather shouted, "Don't!" Being ten years old, Clay thought himself wise enough to make big decisions. Two years younger, Heather knew she was more responsible because she was the one who listened. Mom had said to keep the entry locked. Even so, Clay flicked the latch, turned the knob, and swung the door inward.

A man stared down at him.

Heather backed into the corridor by the stairs, ready to

run to her bedroom. Anger buzzed her bones. Clay was *such* a nincompoop.

Cool air breezed into the house along with a pungent smell like the sports shed by the school gymnasium. The man was almost a foot taller than her five-foot-tall brother. His shaggy brown hair was unkempt and unwashed, his skin pale, grimy, almost gray. An enormous beard grew down to the middle of his chest. His greenish denim overalls had clearly once been blue, and his red-and-black-checkered shirt looked almost worn through. Something about the man was familiar—the way his long nose curved slightly to the left. The mischievous tilt of his thick eyebrows reminded Heather of her father. In fact, the man looked like he might have *been* their father. When the man smiled, the corners of his brown eyes crinkled.

"Clay?" His voice sounded like stones being crushed under a shoe. "Heather?" He tried to cross the threshold, but Clay, impressively, held up his hands to stop him.

How does he know our names?

"Who are you?" Clay asked with some force.

"I don't mean to scare you," said the man. "It's just . . . I haven't seen you in what feels like a lifetime."

"We've met before? When?"

The man cleared his throat. "We're getting ahead of ourselves."

Heather thought to run to the kitchen, to call someone who might help.

"I have something to tell you," the man went on, clasping his hands. "You're not going to believe me. But I swear, my story is true. And you need to hear it, whether you want to or not."

"My dad'll be home any second," Heather called out from the hallway.

"I'm not here to hurt anyone," said the man. "I only want to help."

"We don't need help," said Clay, pushing at the door. The man put out his foot, stopping it with a toe of his black leather boots.

"My name is Tommy," the man blurted out. "I'm your little brother."

Heather almost laughed, but something stopped her—the memory of how Tommy had quit crying suddenly, a little over two minutes ago. She glanced toward their bedrooms. A shadow had moved across the sun, and it was suddenly dark up there.

"Check the crib." The man pulled his foot back, and Clay slammed the door shut. "I'll wait." The voice came through the glass.

"Clay?" Heather whispered, frightened.

Clay turned the lock.

The two raced up the stairs.

Tommy's crib was empty. Heather peered underneath. A doll she'd never noticed before was lying against the wall, just out of reach. It was made of cloth, with black-button eyes and a stitched red grin. Clay looked in the closet, tossing clothes out onto the floor. "Tommy!" he shouted.

"He was *just* here," said Heather.

They searched the other bedrooms, then rushed through the rooms downstairs. Heather opened the door to the basement, calling to her little brother again. She and Clay crept down the steps, pulling the string for the bulb at the bottom. There were boxes stacked along the walls. Shadows upon shadows. Piles of laundry beside the washer and dryer. They tossed around musty underwear and socks in a frantic whirlwind.

"Did *he* take him?" Heather asked. "The man at the door?"

"How?"

"Maybe he's not alone."

Carefully, the two climbed back up to the hallway, then dashed to the kitchen. If the man was still at the door, they didn't want him to see where they'd gone. Heather dialed her father's office. When he picked up, she told him what was happening.

He'd never sounded so panicked. "Hide in the cupboard. Don't come out, no matter what."

"But *Tommy*!" Heather pleaded.

"I'm getting the police," said her father. The line clicked off. He'd hung up on her! She grabbed Clay and pulled him into the cupboard with the mop and the broom, and then closed the daylight away.

Minutes later there was a knocking from the front of the house. Heather gripped Clay's slick hand tightly, afraid to move, blink, breathe. He opened the cupboard and peered into the hallway. "It's the police."

Through the front window, Heather saw someone in uniform.

Lights flashed at the curb. Heather watched as officers put the bearded man in handcuffs. He looked strangely at ease, as if he'd expected this to happen. She cried as officers went through the house. A woman with a black ponytail and a navy blue pantsuit arrived. Detective Johnson. In the living room, she asked questions.

When their parents came home, it was all hugs and tears, wide eyes and loud voices.

"The man says that *he's* Tommy," Heather said. It was frustrating to explain again and again what had happened.

Then she remembered the weird doll under Tommy's crib. When Detective Johnson asked an officer to check, they said there was nothing there.

Heather scowled. She was sure she'd seen it.

At least, she'd *thought* she was sure.

Unless . . .

Maybe she wasn't sure at all.

The police put out an alert, instructed the family to stay put. Heather watched through the window as they loaded the bearded man into the back of a car. Their neighbors stood on their front porches, arms crossed, as officers made rounds, asking questions.

Inside their house, time ceased to exist. Mom and Dad were placing calls, trying to keep it together. It felt suddenly as if Heather and Clay weren't there anymore, as if they were no longer part of this story.

After sunset, Detective Johnson asked that the family come to the station. The bearded man insisted that his name was Tommy. And *this* Tommy, the adult version, told Detective Johnson that he would only speak with Heather and Clay. She said it was highly unusual to allow a suspect to meet with victims, children no less, but the quicker they got answers from him, the better. Mom and Dad were adamant against it at first, but then agreed if they could stay with the kids.

In the interrogation room, the bearded man was cuffed to a desk. When they entered the room, the bearded man's face lit up, and he exclaimed, "Mama! Daddy!" Super weird, but no one said anything. The family sat opposite the man, far away, against the wall. Detective Johnson stood in one corner. By the ceiling, a small device emitted a red light.

"Well?" said Dad.

The bearded man leaned toward them. "I have a story to tell."

It went something like this:

That afternoon, Tommy had not wanted to lie down for his nap. He'd screamed and cried and rattled the bars of his big-boy bed, hoping his brother and sister would take him away. But they didn't come. So he kept crying.

The little people appeared so suddenly, Tommy forgot how upset he was. They stared up, shiny button eyes catching what little light seeped in through the curtains. Their smiles were red stitches. He'd seen people like this before. His mama kept one on her bed, between Daddy's pillow and hers. She'd had it ever since she was little like Tommy. Mama called it Rag-Doll.

"Raddoll," Tommy said to the little people.

"Yes," said one of them. A floppy girl with loops of orange yarn hair. "Raddolls. We're here to play with you, Tommy. Do you want to play?"

"Want to," Tommy answered.

Two of the Raddolls, purple hair and black, climbed the sides of his big-boy bed and unlatched the slatted siding. Tommy jumped to the floor.

The Raddolls told Tommy to follow them. Then, something silly happened. Something like magic. There was a ripping sound. And in the middle of Tommy's bedroom, a doorway appeared. Only it didn't look like a regular door. No, this looked like the entrance to a deep, dark cave, like in the Aladdin storybook whose pages Mama let him flip. Inside the door was dark and spooky, and Tommy wondered if there might be a genie.

But the Raddolls looked so happy, Tommy went with them.

"A new world," said the Raddoll with the orange loopy hair. This world looked just like the old world. There was his bedroom. There was also the rest of the house, which the Raddolls let him explore as much as he liked.

Here, the clock on his bedroom wall didn't tick. The sun didn't move in the sky. And the wind didn't blow. Cars didn't drive loudly down the street. And no one came and went. It was only Tommy and the Raddolls.

For a while, that was fine.

They played for a long time. There was lots of pretending in the new world. They pretended they were doggies running in a pack. They were pirates who rescued mermaids from angry dolphins. They were astronauts floating around a pink planet.

Since the clocks didn't tick and the sun didn't move and no one came and went, Tommy almost forgot about his family.

"Where's Mama and Daddy?" he asked his new friends. "Where's Clay and Hezzuh?"

"They're around," said the orange hair Raddoll. "You'll see them any minute now. Aren't you sleepy?"

Tommy started to get mad. They wanted him to take a nap. He fussed and moaned, but that tired him out, so he lay down on the floor, and the Raddolls snuggled up next to him. Real close. And before he knew it, they were all fast asleep.

When he woke, the Raddolls were ready to play again. But Tommy wanted to see his family. "Any minute now," they told him.

They told him that for a long, long time.

Tommy grew bigger. Smarter. Any minute now was taking forever.

He began to read the storybooks himself, and when he was hungry, he grabbed food from the kitchen while the Raddolls watched. When the cupboards ran low, the Raddolls brought more, from neighboring houses. From the books, he got clues about how to brush his teeth and clip his fingernails and use the toilet and wash up. From the books, he started to understand how the world was supposed to be. He gathered all the pictures of Mama and Daddy and Clay and Heather and kept them in his bedroom so he could remember their faces and dream of a time they'd be together again.

What was important to the Raddolls was that when Tommy slept, they piled against his body, keeping him warm. Once, when he woke, he noticed a tear at the neck of the one with green hair. The stuffing inside was spilling out; only it wasn't stuffing. It was more like sand. Or ash. Black and clinging and swirly—almost like smoke, but . . . not. When the Raddolls noticed him looking, they smuggled Green Hair away, and when he came back, the tear had been sewn up.

Tommy grew bigger. Smarter.

Sometimes, he wandered outside the neighborhood. The Raddolls always followed. Tommy would enter houses, find new books to read and new things to learn. He discovered road atlases and world maps and wondered if there would ever be a time when he might discover these places for himself.

Maybe.

If the Raddolls let him.

They'd stopped playing, stopped pretending, long ago. Their cloth bodies were becoming ratty. Cotton pills forming on their clothes. Drool stains and dirt on their faces and limbs. Whenever there was a tear, that black, ashy not-smoke leaked out.

Tommy started to think this was strange, the stuff inside them. From his books, he knew that his own body was filled with bones and blood and meat, items that kept him moving, breathing, seeing, thinking. He hadn't read anything anywhere about how the stuffing in the Raddolls might do the same for them.

They weren't *little* people after all.

Eventually, the Raddolls quit repairing themselves. This was around the time they stopped speaking. Lazy. Complacent. Tommy was too big, and they had nothing more to share. All the stories had been told. All the games had been played. When the black stuff came out, they just shoved it back inside. Later, they stripped away their skins entirely. The black stuffing kept the shape of their former bodies, but it was not solid. If Tommy tried to touch them, his hand went through. The most awful part was the teeth—circular rows would float around in the black stuffing, sometimes appearing, sometimes not. It became more and more difficult to sleep with the Raddolls piled next to him. Without their skins, he could feel their little mouths, and a pressure, like suckling.

He came to believe that any minute now was a lie. Tommy needed to go, to set off on a path he'd charted in a road atlas from his daddy's study.

He prepared a duffel with clothes and cans of food and a picture of his family. Then, lying on the floor, he yawned and stretched, which usually brought the Raddolls scampering. As if for a feeding. When they were all around him, he reached under the old crib and brought out a vacuum machine. He switched it on, and before the Raddolls could run, he managed to suck them inside. With the Raddolls trapped in the vacuum, he grabbed his bag and went out into the daylit world.

He traveled far. Saw many sights he'd only read about in books. Rivers and bridges. Cliffs and gullies. He encountered plants with leaves whose shapes were like stars and hearts and hands. He climbed mountains covered in snow, crossed ponds whose surfaces refused to ripple, even after he tossed large rocks into them. He found new towns, some of them much larger than others, some with houses that reached up and up and up. There were rooms filled with books, where he liked to camp and read, and other buildings where he found food to take with him. Before moving on, he'd check the road atlas so he always knew where he'd been, and also where he was headed next.

Tommy grew bigger, smarter, even as the sun remained lodged in its place in the sky and the puffy clouds surrounding it were static, like in photographs. Long after he'd left the house where he'd last seen his family, he came to a cottage at the bottom of a lonely road. To his surprise, he saw a person out front—a woman in a ratty sweater and a full skirt—hunched down in a lush garden.

Was she the first real person he'd encountered in all this time?

She called herself Mei, and she invited him in for tea. Only after he'd stepped into her cottage did he worry he'd made a mistake. In the corners of her kitchen, half a dozen skinless Raddolls sat and stared with their eyeless faces, looking as floppy as his mother's old Rag-Doll. Mei saw his hesitation, then asked him, "Where are your Dusters?"

Dusters? Oh, right. The Raddolls.

"I left them a long time ago," he said.

He didn't want to say what he'd done with the vacuum machine, in case these ones were listening.

Mei was surprised. "They're probably following you," she said.

But Tommy told her he hadn't seen them in what felt like forever.

She grunted, sounding doubtful. She boiled the water,

grabbed herbs from a jar, and placed handfuls into a couple of mugs. "It's not often I've encountered others like us," she explained as the tea steeped. "Only a few times since they took me." She glanced at the Raddolls in the room. Their circles of teeth peeked out from their stuffing and then receded again. "Why did you leave them?" she asked. "They need us."

"I wanted to find Mama and Daddy and Clay and Heather. And ... and I didn't like the way they felt when we slept."

"Ah, yes. There's that." She handed him one of the mugs, nodded for him to take a sip. She said, "There is a way out, I heard about once from a traveler like you."

"Out?"

"Out of this world. Back to our place and time. In the city. Hundreds of miles south, where the river meets the ocean. That's where the big one eats. It likes the energy there."

"What is the big one?" Tommy asked.

"Mm," said Mei. She lowered her voice. "The other traveler called it THE VOID. An entity who makes the doors. Portals. These little ones"—she indicated the lazy Raddolls, or Dusters—"they follow it, steal what they need. They keep us ... and feed."

"Feed on what?" he asked, even though he felt he knew.

"Our warmth. Our energy. Our ... soul. Whatever you want to call it. The secret thing inside us that keeps us alive ... It helps them thrive. And we ... we grow old," she said.

She sipped her own tea, then went on, "The Dusters know

how to close the smaller doors. But the bigger doors . . . THE VOID's? I hear they remain open."

"So there's a way home? To my family?"

"If you're willing to make the journey."

"I am," said Tommy. He thought. "Will you come with me?"

Mei said no. Her body was too frail. The road was long, the city too far. She had her garden and her home, and she was mostly happy here. She didn't mind the Dusters' teeth. She was used to it.

"But aren't you lonely?" Tommy asked.

"I'm not alone," said Mei. Her lips parted into a crooked smile.

Tommy took the road south, hiking under the constant sun. In his books, in the stories, he'd read about night and dark, but he couldn't remember what that felt like. He thought of THE VOID. Whenever he tried to imagine what it might look like, his mind put up a wall.

Eventually, he came to the city. The horizon made of spikes made him think of castles and dragons and politics and money—bits of fantasy that had never been part of his life. A tunnel dipped under a wide body of water. When he emerged, he felt a kind of tugging in his belly, and he understood that if he followed the sensation, it would lead him where he needed to go. Buildings were so tall, they blocked out the sun. Across a massive bridge, the sensation grew stronger. He came to a driveway and a gate, spires reaching up and up and up, like the buildings he'd passed on the way here. Gravestones poked out of the grass. At the top of a hill, he saw the crevice. Its edges shimmered. This one was enormous—many times the size of the door he'd seen in his bedroom when he was little.

As he approached, he noticed movement at the sides of his vision.

His Raddolls stepped out from behind the graves.

"Found you," said the one with orange hair. She'd remade her skin of cloth, sewn that red smile back onto her face.

He ignored her and ran toward the opening. Tommy was bigger now. Smarter. She couldn't fool him again.

Others appeared. Green hair. Purple. Black. More and more. They chased him past the gravestones. Grabbed at his overalls, climbed his legs, hung from his arms. They bit down, their circular jaws latching onto his skin, sucking and sucking and sucking. He spun. Some went flying. The others he ripped off and flung aside.

He was nearly at the great crevice, the one Mei had claimed was left behind by THE VOID, the portal, the passage that could not close, when Orange Hair stepped out in front of him. He almost kicked her out of his way, but she said something that made him stop in his tracks:

"Heather."

Then she said:

"Clay."

She stared up at him with her black button eyes. "We'll find our way back there. We'll take them instead of you."

Tommy shuddered, thinking of his siblings. How could he put them through what he'd already lived? Maybe Mei had been right to stay put. But that tugging in his belly was almost unbearable.

The passage wanted him to step forward.

To enter, as if this thing were a mouth and he was some tasty morsel.

Without another thought, that's what he did.

The bearded man was quiet for a moment. He considered the family, who'd listened to his tale.

Heather saw tears edging on his lower eyelids, but he managed to hold them back. She didn't know what to think.

"I had to tell you this," said the man. "So you all know what's coming."

"We're done," said Dad, glancing at Detective Johnson.

Before the family left the room, the bearded man called out, "Clay. Heather. Please. Beware."

Heather felt a sudden urge to rush over, embrace the man, squeeze him tightly, despite his stink, but her mother ushered her out the door.

Later, at home, the parents sat in the living room, unable to bring themselves to try and sleep. They'd sent both Clay and Heather upstairs to brush their teeth, wash up, and ready themselves for bed.

From the top of the stairs, Heather heard her mother crying. Her father said, "The police will call. Just you wait. They'll bring him home. Any minute now."

Lying in the darkness of her room, Heather tossed and turned. Clay had said the bearded man was wild to expect any of them to believe his tale.

Since Heather was the sibling who listened, she couldn't stop herself from considering what the story might mean. If it was *only* a story, maybe a clue was hidden inside. Maybe the man really *did* know where Tommy was, but he couldn't say directly. There was something called *metaphor* that Heather's teacher, Mr. Waters, had taught them about a few months back. Sometimes words had meanings other than what was in the dictionary. Sometimes stories represented something bigger than what was on the page. Mr. Waters had even made the class come up with some of their own.

In her bed, Heather struggled to imagine what the bearded man's metaphor could be. Or how it would lead them to Tommy. She thought of the story of the man at the door, of the life he claimed to have led, and she imagined her own life to come. How it would change after this day. After this night.

Her mind conjured up what might be in store: the people she might meet, the things she might see, the places where she might travel, the love she might find. And what she might lose.

Restless, Heather left her room, went down the hall to Tommy's. The police had said to not touch anything, but she swung her leg over the side of Tommy's big-boy bed anyway. The mattress groaned as she curled her body upon it. She glanced at the clock on Tommy's wall. Its second hand was marked with a star that chased the larger hands with a sun and a moon. *Tick, tick, tick.* The sound was a comfort.

Here, in the dark, she thought of the bearded man's warning. Of the Raddolls. Of the portals. Of how time might stop the sun from moving across the sky. She pressed her face into her brother's pillow and breathed in the scent of him. There was a sweetness inside that no metaphor could have described. Her tears wet the pillowcase, and she shivered.

Heather woke with a start. There were swishing noises in the dark. Like fabric brushing against fabric.

She sat up, stared into the shadows, looking through the bed's slats. "Tommy?" she whispered.

The sounds stopped.

Holding her breath, Heather reached for the lamp. Her ears buzzed, and she realized Tommy's sun and moon and stars clock had stopped ticking. Her fingers found the switch. Dim light poured across Tommy's blue rug.

On the floor, not far from the closed bedroom door, Heather

noticed the doll she remembered seeing under the mattress that afternoon. Its orange hair was clumps of tangled yarn. A green gingham dress came down just beyond its knees. Its black button eyes stared at the ceiling, its stitched red smile twitching, as if ready to say hello.

CLOSED FOR THE SEASON

Peter Mackenzie watched from inside the darkened shop as the car parked at the curb. A family climbed out and made their way down the concrete path beside the building, heading toward the creek at the rear. There were a dad and a mom and two kids who looked to be around his age. Maybe eleven or twelve. When they came to the chain, they read the sign—NO ENTRY. THIS TRAIL IS CLOSED FOR THE SEASON—then stepped over and made their way down the stone steps.

Feeling his cheeks growing warm, Peter clicked his tongue.

The River Walk had been a tourist destination for a few years. From here, the trail ran alongside the creek at the back of the buildings and emerged into a small park next to the town hall a half mile down. After the village had fixed up the trail, people flocked to the area, not just for the pretty hike, but for the quaint cafés, bookstores, and secondhand shops like the one Peter's parents owned.

His father had named it Curiosities because it was filled with all sorts of strange things, not only old clothes and furniture that people didn't want anymore, but books with weird titles, mirrors whose glass had turned black, hand-built clay busts of bald vampires with twisted faces, diaries of children who claimed to be friends with the monsters under their beds, apothecary jars filled with dried purple flowers and labeled GOBLIN'S TONGUE.

Sometimes, Peter grew fond of certain items that came to the shop, and when they were sold, he couldn't help but feel sad. His recent favorites were an illustrated bestiary by an author called October Bowen and a peculiar-looking seashell, red and glossy with sharp purple spikes that stuck out all over like teeth—both of which his father had acquired from an auction a couple weeks ago.

The past year had been busy. Something that Mom and Dad used to complain about was how village taxes were inching higher. Peter didn't understand fully, but he'd vowed to learn someday since, eventually, he'd have to pay them too.

Following the rules felt imperative.

He rushed to the back of the store, to the window that overlooked the creek and the walkway. The family now stood gawking at the beauty of the barren forest and rolling hills in the distance, showing no shame for climbing over the chain and ignoring the *very specific* sign. In his bedroom on the second floor, Peter removed the illustrated bestiary and the spiky red seashell from under his bed, his hands tingling, then positioned himself at his desk so he could watch the family as they ventured along the winding creek.

The mother snapped pictures of bare branches and churning water. When she turned to focus the camera up at Peter, she jolted in surprise, then raised her hand in a nervous wave. The father also turned to look, squinting into the slanted light of the afternoon, his breath turning to fog in the cold air. Peter smiled and waved back but whispered, *"This is simply not allowed."*

He flipped October Bowen's bestiary open and turned to a random page. The book was a kind of encyclopedia, with several rhyming entries and detailed watercolor paintings scattered across each spread. The one that caught his eye today was for a creature known as Jenny Greenteeth. The illustration showed a woman submerged at a river's edge. Her eyes were black marbles. Her hair was river grass, clinging to her skull. A bony arm stretched from the water, fingers like elongated claws, reaching toward the ankle of a dopey-looking child who was not paying attention. Peter balanced the book on his lap, then lifted the seashell to his lips like a musical instrument. A familiar numbing sensation spread out across his jaw. He exhaled and a low tone sounded. It rattled his eardrums, and for a moment, his vision blurred. (He was used to this by now.) When he could see properly again, he returned to the Jenny Greenteeth entry and read it aloud:

Her skin is made of rotting leaves.
Her bones are made of sticks.
Her hair is moss and twine and string,
Her voice, bat song and cricket clicks.

When he finished, he thought hard about these people who'd snuck onto the River Walk. The dad. The mom. The two kids, his own age. Then, he did what he always did in moments like this. He waited.

Whenever he considered his life, Peter recognized two incidents that made him see the world in his own way.

The first occurred during catechism class in the basement of the local church. The teacher, Mrs. Tucker, was a kind woman who often gave her students leeway during colorful discussions that frequently veered off topic. On the night in question—don't ask how—the issue of athletic support gear came up. A girl named Gwen, who frequently pretended to be almost foolishly naive, called out in a squeaky voice, "What's a *jockey strap*?" The reaction from the class was swift and loud—screams of laughter, pounding on desks, general bafflement that someone would dare say such a thing in a holy place like this. Mrs. Tucker's face went red, her eyes wide, hands raised in a pleading gesture for everyone to JUST. CALM. DOWN.

It wasn't long before the matron was standing in the doorway in her smart black skirt suit. Sister Janet's wimple covered her hair and neck, and she was glowering. Immediately the class was quiet. "Who was laughing?" Her voice boomed into the small space. "Raise your hand."

Regretfully, Peter stuck his hand in the air, along with fifteen others. The only one who didn't was Gwen. Technically, she hadn't laughed at all, though Peter was certain she *had* meant to be funny.

"Get up, all of you," said Sister Janet, tossing Mrs. Tucker a look of disgust. The class (minus Gwen) followed the nun to her office next door. One by one, Sister Janet made them call their parents to confess what they'd done.

As Peter dialed, his throat constricted and his eyes stung. When his mother answered, he was barely able to get the words out. "Sister Janet wants you to know I was laughing in class."

After a moment, sounding amused, she replied, "Please tell Sister Janet that you're sorry." Peter did, but Sister Janet's reply was not what he'd expected. When you asked God for forgiveness, He always granted it, no matter what, if you truly repented. And yet the matron growled at him, *"It's a little late for that."*

He spent the rest of the night considering this. Sometimes it was TOO LATE for an apology? This news terrified him—wiggled in his brain like a worm. This wasn't what he thought he knew.

What else did he not know?

The second incident occurred at the beginning of the school year. Mrs. Handschuh was that day's substitute English teacher. When Mrs. Handschuh told them the reading assignment, Peter got to it straightaway. Before long, he'd finished, so he took out a novel and read quietly at his desk.

Annoyed, Mrs. Handschuh raised her voice. Scolded him for *not focusing on the task at hand*.

Peter didn't know how to tell her that he'd completed the *task at hand*, so he reopened his textbook and read the entire passage again, slower this time, focusing on each and every word. Still, he made it through before the end of the bell. He didn't believe she could possibly expect him to sit and stare into space, so once again, he took his novel from his book bag.

A moment later, the substitute snatched the novel away, then said with a quiet venom, "This is simply not allowed."

When he explained to the principal, Mr. Dickinson, what had happened, the principal sighed and told him to take a seat on the bench in the school office to wait out the end of the period. He fought to catch his breath, but understood he'd been given a reprieve. It hadn't been like with Sister Janet: *A LITTLE LATE FOR THAT.*

It felt nice to be heard. To be understood. By someone with great authority. Before the end of the school day, Peter returned to Mr. Dickinson and told him that if he ever needed help with anything, he was the kid to do it.

This started Peter's stint as a hall monitor. He didn't care that his classmates called him *narc* and *loser*. The important thing was that the grown-ups saw him follow the rules, knew he was a trustworthy, good person. Peter never wanted to feel that throat-closing, weak-kneed, prickle-skin sensation of getting in trouble ever again.

Within weeks, Peter focused on the junk shop too, helping organize the curiosities into groups, pricing items and then logging them in the binder under the register. He especially enjoyed helping his father catalog new arrivals, which is how he came into contact with the red seashell with the purple spikes and the illustrated bestiary. The first time he held the seashell in his hands, the tips of his fingers tingled, and he heard a voice in his head—not quite his own—which said loudly, gruffly: *MINE*. The illustrations in the bestiary were almost as striking as the mollusk's exoskeleton, and whenever he looked through them, they seemed to move slightly.

In his room, he hid them both under his bed.

Outside, the screaming lasted for less than a minute, then quiet descended again. From the window, Peter saw the creek below run red, but that could have been the late light reflecting off the water. He raised the sash and peered outside, leaning slightly past the ledge, trying to catch a glimpse of the River Walk.

The dad, mom, and two kids were gone now.

Good.

He reached again for the seashell, to press his lips to it a second time and blow that final dark note, to finish what he'd begun and close the door he'd opened, sending away the creature it had summoned. But the shell slipped from his grip and hit the floor with a horrifying crunch. Peter retrieved it, cradling the shell in his arms.

One of the purple spikes had snapped off and was lying next to the illustrated bestiary, which had fallen from his lap.

Reassuring himself that everything would be fine, Peter brought the shell to his mouth and exhaled. No note sounded. What came out was a harsh echoing sound, like distant ocean waves.

No. No. No!

He would not allow himself to get upset.

There was a way to fix this.

In the hall closet, he located a tube of epoxy. He spread the adhesive onto the broken spike and fit it to the hole from which it had snapped. Applying pressure, he held it tight. Outside, the wind knocked through the bare winter branches. After the recommended time, he let go of the spike. He gave it a shake, but it stayed firmly in place.

Once more, he held the shell to his lips. This time a tone sounded, but it was different than before. Higher pitched. Almost like shrieking. The fuzzy feeling he'd always gotten when he touched the shell was missing. And his mouth and jaw didn't have that soft ache like they were supposed to. Still, Peter gathered up the illustrated bestiary and the red shell, and then grabbed a pen from his desk drawer before heading downstairs to finish the job.

He stepped out onto the shop's small porch. The season's chill seeped through his shirt, but Peter didn't pay attention to the goose bumps. He focused on the car parked at the curb—the black sedan that belonged to the family. Placing the shell on the top step, he sat and then located the entry for *Jenny Greenteeth* in the bestiary. There, he jotted the license plate, and because he did not know the family's names, he wrote down, *A MOM, A DAD, AND TWO KIDS, MY AGE*, just like he'd done with names of his neighbors and townspeople throughout the rest of the book. He also wrote, *THEY IGNORED THE SIGN THAT SAYS "CLOSED FOR THE SEASON."*

Way back, on the first night he'd shoved the shell and the bestiary beneath his bed, his dreams had been strange. Voices gave instructions and told him rules and shared secrets. He saw teeth and tentacles and tusks, scales and tails and breath that was fire and ice. When he woke the next morning, he felt different—still himself, mostly, but it was as if he knew more, and better. As he stared at the shell, his dreams came flooding back, and he felt new. He felt . . . *righteous*. Was that even a word? The dreams continued to come, and with them, a desire . . . not unlike the one he'd had as hall monitor.

On the porch, Peter flipped through the bestiary, considering all that he'd done.

Beside the entry for Griffin, he'd scrawled, *MR. CONSIDINE. DROVE WRONG WAY UP ONE-WAY STREET.* He recalled the shape that had descended from the sky just after he'd blown into the shell, that amalgam of furred haunches and silvery wings, a beak like a blade, and the talons that clutched the roof of Mr. Considine's Volkswagen before lifting off—the man shrieking from inside—and disappearing over the jagged pine horizon.

In the margins next to the picture for Kraken, he'd noted the name *JESSE MARKSMAN* (an older boy who'd never been very kind to him). *SMOKED A CIGARETTE WITHIN TWENTY FEET OF THE ORPHEUM THEATER ENTRANCE.* Afterward, a colossal indigo tentacle had popped the manhole cover from out of the middle of the street, sent it flying fifteen feet before it landed on the double yellow line. When the tip of the creature's arm wrapped around Jesse's thigh and dragged him underground, Peter felt a smug satisfaction. *That's what you get!*

One of the bestiary's final entries was for something called THE VOID, and he'd used that one to take care of a couple of city people who'd run across Main Street outside of the crosswalk painted at the corner. *CITY PEOPLE. JAYWALKED.* There'd been a blink of shadow, curls of smoke or mist, and then the two were simply . . . gone. Along with a small chunk of sidewalk.

There were more. *Many more.* The number of rules that one could break around here seemed countless—almost too many for a single kid with a seashell and an encyclopedia of monsters to keep up with.

Almost.

Now the light had settled into a beautiful post-sunset purple, and high cirrus clouds streaked the sky with gray. In recent days, the town had become almost silent. Traffic was lighter than usual. When tourists saw how most of the storefronts were dark, they kept driving, heading to the next quaint town a dozen miles up the county highway. This was concerning. If the shop did not continue to pull a profit, Peter wouldn't be able to keep the doors open, especially now that his parents were gone. He flipped to the entry where he'd written, *MOM AND DAD. ARGUED DURING DINNERTIME.* This he'd scrawled next to the name of a kind of creature that was still difficult for him to comprehend. According to the book, a Time-Snatcher was a type of hobgoblin, made up of shifting black sand and moveable teeth. He couldn't be sure what the thing *really* looked like, because when they'd arrived, he hadn't caught a glimpse. His parents had been watching television in the den, perched on opposite sides of the couch, still mad at each other... And then... they weren't there anymore. Peter had gone to bed feeling an awful guilt. But by morning, it was easy to brush off. He'd made himself breakfast and then showered and gone to school.

On the porch, Peter closed the book, tucked it under his arm, and stood. He picked up the seashell and examined the seam where he'd glued the broken spike. He felt nervous that its tone had been different when he'd blown a second time, to send away Jenny Greenteeth. But the important thing was he'd followed the rules.

That had to count for something, right?

Inside, he locked the door and turned on the hallway light.

A crash came from the back of the shop. Peter stiffened. Was there an intruder? A burglar? He placed the shell and the book on a side table and stepped through the wide entry that led into the parlor room. His parents' "curiosities" were stacked so high, he couldn't see what had made the noise. He sidled through the shop carefully.

Near the window overlooking the creek, a shadow shifted, then vanished. Several broken panes glittered on the floor. Peter saw movement in the edges of his vision. Twilight shadow spread from the corners of the room, and a figure emerged from the darkness between two bookshelves.

Startled, Peter stumbled back, landing on the shattered glass. The pain in his palms was insignificant.

He recognized her of course: the creature from the bestiary, Jenny Greenteeth, whom he'd sent after *A MOM, A DAD, AND TWO KIDS, MY AGE.*

"It was an accident." His voice filled with a fear he wished he could simply send away. "I didn't mean to break it. The shell slipped from my hands. I glued it back on. You can barely tell."

Jenny crawled farther out from between the bookcases. Her elbows pointed toward the ceiling. Her arms were as thin as fallen branches. Her skin was an emerald color, and so dark in some places it resembled the sky on a starless night. Her cheeks were sunken and hollow. A couple dead leaves were stuck to her forehead, nearly slipping down over one eye. Long hair hung from her scalp in sporadic clumps. But it wasn't quite hair, was it? More like weeds dragged up from the bottom of a pool. She kept her chest low to the ground, but her head was focused forward, her empty gaze drawing Peter in. His back pressed against the wall beneath the window.

Jenny released a soft hiss as she came closer, only inches away now. Peter closed the back of his throat so he wouldn't have to breathe in the sweet smell of decay. She tilted her chin up toward what was left of the daylight. Between her black eyes, two teardrop-shaped slits pulsated with muddled breath. She dragged herself toward him.

Peter was tempted to kick out, but he still had a chance to explain. They were on the *same side*, after all.

When she parted the black gash of her lips, he finally saw Jenny's long, needlelike teeth. They were indeed green—vibrant and neon, as if lit from within—curving inward toward her writhing worm-tongue. As she widened her jaw, her teeth pushed outward like extended cat claws.

He felt hot tears. Something had broken inside him—a spell?—and the impact of what he'd done hit him like a rock to his temple. "I'm sorry," he cried, begging. "I'm sorry for all of it."

Jenny Greenteeth reached out, placed her hand on his throat, the sharp tips of her fingers digging into his skin. Her dark eyes flashed with fury, but the edges of her mouth curled into an amused smile. With a voice that sounded as soft as night and as harsh as the crunching of bones, she answered him. *"A LITTLE . . . LATE . . . FOR THAT . . ."*

GILBERT AT THE LAST STATION

The train wheels ground against the rail. Gilbert leaned hard, grabbing the satchel before it could fly off the seat. The car came to a rough halt, and the doors snapped open. Speakers chimed and then announced, "THIS STOP IS . . . *ALDRIDGE PLACE.*" He dashed onto the brightly lit platform, the image of Jenny's green teeth lingering in his mind.

Catching a glimpse of the graffiti inside the car, his skin went all gooseflesh. Its message was now complete.

NOVEMBER'S DOOR.

That's what all this had been about. For the magician's doorway to open fully, Gilbert had to listen to the thirteen tales created by the students at the Bureau of Black Holes and Supernovas.

This was where they led him.

The station name was spelled out in tile on the platform wall. He'd never come across a stop called Aldridge Place on this line before. In fact, he was certain it didn't exist. At least, not in this city.

Gilbert expected the subway doors to shut, for the train to rush off and leave him here alone, but they remained open. He took the platform steps two by two, then ran, his mind creating monsters at his heels. Through gleaming passageways. Past cage-like turnstiles. And as he ran, his mind raced too. Not only had he unlocked November's Door, but something else as well. Something larger. The connections among all the stories—and the library book still tucked firmly in his satchel—blurred together. Finally, daylight slanted down the final flight to the street.

Above was blue sky, the air warm on his face. Coming up the stairs, he saw green leaves high overhead. Stepping into a different season, he unzipped his coat, shoved his cap into his pocket.

He tried to recall the first tale from the first tape. Had Tony also found himself at a strange train station? There was a gravel road in a forest clearing, a stone path, a massive house, all angular alcoves and sharp peaks, storm-colored shingles, and a slate roof coated in yellow-green moss. To reach the entry, he'd have to pass under a trellis of twisty vines and through a garden of flowers and stalks and pods that were unlike any plants Gilbert had ever encountered in the city. They were all wild. But one stood out—a vaguely sinister-looking purple blossom.

Why is that one so familiar?

Gilbert shuddered—too many stories were floating in his mind. Keeping his thoughts straight right now was a battle.

A breeze whispered. A door slammed. Someone was standing on the porch—a bulk of darkness, like the figure in Ant's hospital room. "There you are," a deep voice called out. "He's been waiting for you."

Gilbert wound the satchel's straps around one wrist as if it were a weapon.

"Best you just come in," said the shape. They wore dingy black jeans and a dark hoodie. Their eyes were dark too, as was their buzzed hair and whisper of a mustache. They paused before adding, "He can help your brother."

Shadows threatened the edges of Gilbert's vision as the person opened the door. Inside, he struggled to tamp down anger. Fear.

The entry hall reminded him of museums. Wood paneling. Marble floors. Potted ferns sat on stone pedestals. The walls were papered with deep greens and blues—all ocean depths and chilly nights. Through an expansive doorway, there appeared a parlor with tufted black couches and chairs edged with golden fringe, Persian rugs of dizzying geometrical design, lush, ruby-velvet drapes. An icy chandelier cast rainbows from a massive height.

"This way, child."

Near the front window, a man was sitting in a high-backed

chair, the wings of which spread in a grand gesture, like arms calling Gilbert forward. Whatever he had expected of November—the architect behind the tapes and the tales, the voice on the red phone, *the magician*—the small person here was the opposite. He wore a brown tweed suit, his paunch bunching against his vest and a gold watch chain glinting across his middle. His bald head was pale, his long black beard streaked with gray. Wildly overgrown eyebrows tweaked out just above wire spectacles, the thick glass of which gave him a curious, owl-like appearance.

"You found me," he said, standing. He was barely as tall as Gilbert. "It must have been quite a journey." The voice was different than the one in the ice cream truck tale—the one that had come from the red phone—higher pitched and genteel. Gilbert said nothing, simply swung the satchel over his shoulder. The man extended his hand. "November Bowen. Though I'd wager a clever kid like you would have already gathered that for yourself."

Clever kid felt like both a compliment and an insult. "You can help my brother?" Gilbert asked, no-nonsense.

"I'm sure we can come to an agreement about that." November continued to hold out his hand. "Please, sit." He gestured to a loveseat. When Gilbert hesitated, he added, "I won't take no for an answer." This last bit sounded almost like a threat. Gilbert sat, sinking into the pillow-soft cushion, clasping the leather bag on his lap. "I expect you have questions."

"A few," said Gilbert, his jaw tight. "Your tapes already answered most of them." November tossed his head back and chortled. Amused? Offended?

Gilbert went on, "*Stories are doorways to other worlds?*"

The magician was impressed. "Indeed. And listening to my stories brought you here. I must say, I don't allow many visitors. Some might argue you're quite lucky. See, your life is about to change."

"The only thing I want to change is what happened to my brother."

"Yes, yes, of course. Antonio is not well?"

As if he doesn't know . . .

Gilbert kept his tongue cool. "Ant's in the hospital. Someone found him this morning. All scraped up . . . unconscious. Did . . . did *you* do that to him?"

For the first time, November's genial expression darkened. "I'd say Antonio did it to himself. He'd accepted the gift of working for me. He understood the rules. But then he broke them. That was entirely his decision."

Gilbert's skin went cold. "So then the story was true. The one about the exterminators? You set some rabid animal on him?"

"Rabid animal?" November scoffed. "Hardly."

Gilbert took that as a *yes*. "What do you want from me?"

"Cut to the chase, you mean?" November smiled, his long beard quivering. "Having ambitions such as mine, I've learned I need assistance. I must *delegate*. Which is where you come in. Not many have made it through those tapes. Quite a gauntlet you and Antonio both passed. Usually, this indicates strong character, someone capable of loyalty . . . Usually, but not *always*. Antonio deviated from my rules, and now I require a replacement. If you agree to be that replacement, Gilbert, your brother will make a full recovery."

Gilbert felt his jaw drop. "You're . . . offering me a *job*?"

"Not so much a job as a responsibility."

"Doing what?"

"A little of this. A little of that. I haven't quite decided. You'll be well compensated, I assure you."

Gilbert recalled the job "Tony" had taken in the first story—delivering envelopes that contained names. Names of people who would be . . . *exterminated*. "I won't hurt people," he said.

November's weird little smile grew thin. "I wouldn't ask you to."

The man was lying. In fact, Gilbert realized that *all* of this was a lie, a fabrication, *a story*. The parlor seemed to shiver, like a painting on a veil. He imagined a dank hallway, brick walls, a metal door, a face whose skin was wan, whose eyes were hungry, whose teeth had been ground into sharp points. "What if I say no?"

November scrunched his brow. "I can't imagine you would."

"But what if I do?" Gilbert dared.

"If it's *no*, then I'd be sorry to lose a potential helper. And . . . well . . ." He tented his fingers upon his belly. "You'd lose a brother."

Gilbert couldn't show his fear, but he couldn't stop thinking of the stories—about the mistakes some characters had made, how others had been flung into situations beyond their control. Like it or not, he was one of them now. What terrified him most was that the old man simply did not care.

November stared at Gilbert, waiting for a response.

"The kid on your porch works for you?"

November nodded. "Clay is one of my best."

He thought of the shadowy figure disappearing into the hospital bathroom—*Clay*, he now knew. "Would you teach me . . . magic?"

November sat up, enthused. "If you do well, I shall teach you many things. More than your imagination can conjure."

Something shifted in Gilbert's mind. *Magic* . . . Was it worth considering? For surely there was no denying the magic of this place, of this man. Not only would Gilbert save his brother, but he'd learn what few others ever dreamed of knowing. He thought about Mr. November's rules. Would they be *that* difficult to keep?

Of course they would.

Why else had Ant ended up in such a sorry state?

Gilbert held the satchel in his lap, sensing the tapes

inside, and the player. And the library book, written by October, the magician's sister. And suddenly, he remembered where he'd seen that purple flower in the front garden. *Goblin's Tongue*, from October's book. A plan crystallized. "Can I think about it?"

November sat back, stunned. His silence was terrorizing. After a few long seconds, his eyebrows twitched. Gilbert worried he'd pushed it too far. "I can give you *one day*," said the man. "Let's hope your poor brother lasts that long."

Standing, Gilbert chose his next words wisely. "Can I take these with me?" he asked, holding out the leather satchel and its contents.

The magician rose, almost seemed to hover in the air for a moment before settling to the ground, an act that was clearly meant to hide seething indignation. "I have enough copies of those tapes to last a lifetime," he answered casually, with a sly look that said, *Try and destroy them*. "They're yours."

"Thank you." Gilbert backed toward the entry hall. "And thanks for considering Ant. I'm sure he didn't mean to break your rules."

"And yet here we are." The man's tone was icy now. "Clay will point the way back to the station. I'll be in touch."

Outside, the sun continued to glare down from some summer sky in some other place that Gilbert could only think of as *Elsewhere*. Clay said nothing as Gilbert made his way down the front steps and into the garden.

"The boss said I could pick these," Gilbert mentioned.

Clay glanced sideways through the screen door.

Gilbert opened the satchel and grabbed at the plants, snapping stems, pulling up roots, plucking various blossoms as quickly as he could, shoving them all inside. A bittersweet aroma filled the air—dirt and loam and minerals stirred up from the ground.

"Hey!" Clay shouted. "Stop that."

Gilbert dashed through the emerald trellis to the subway steps.

Down, down, down.

Heavy now, the leather satchel bounced against his ribs.

Footfalls echoed from the corridor behind him.

At the platform, Gilbert raced toward the parked train and swung around the edge of an open doorway, slamming into the seat and scrunching his legs up to his chest. He squeezed his eyes shut, as if that would make him invisible.

In a moment, Clay would find him, rip the satchel away—

"STAND CLEAR OF THE CLOSING DOORS, PLEASE," said the happy voice from the speakers. Chimes rang, and the doors slid shut.

As the train trembled to life, Gilbert glanced out the window, caught a glimpse of shadow descending the steps. By then, the train was speeding up, delivering him from Aldridge Place.

Before the car slipped into darkness, he watched the tiles

that spelled out the station's name flicker, transform, revealing a different name entirely—*Eldritch Place*—confirming his fear that everything he'd seen here had been an illusion, a lie . . .

A story.

GILBERT COMES UPSTAIRS

Gilbert nearly hooted with joy when, moments later, the train pulled into his own station. The platform was packed with people. Upstairs, he stepped onto the sidewalk, into apricot-tinged light and blessedly frigid air. He checked his phone, but the screen was still black. Pushing through the crowd, he made his way to Percy's house.

Mrs. Scala smothered him in a hearty embrace. The greens in the satchel crunched and squeaked. "Where were you?" she asked. "Your grandmother called at least ten times."

Gilbert shivered. "I got stuck on the subway."

Suspicious, Mrs. Scala held him at a distance. *"All night?"*

He tried to not react; this was the first time he'd considered how long the ride had taken. "My phone died."

"Well then . . . let's plug it in."

"Gilbert?" Percy asked from the second-story landing, dressed in blue plaid pajamas and rainbow-striped fuzzy slippers, scrubbing sleep from their eyes. "Are you hungry?"

This question contained so many other questions that Gilbert knew he could only answer once they were alone.

Mrs. Scala was in the kitchen before he could say yes, multitasking bacon, eggs, toast, orange slices, granola, and Greek yogurt. "Call your grandma," she insisted, and handed him her phone.

Of course Grandma Rosemary was angry, his great-aunt Sheila too, even after he gave his excuse about the train being stuck. Gilbert listened patiently to just *how* angry they were. He wanted to tell her about the tapes, the doorways, the magician, the threat, but that would only worry and confuse her more. "How's Ant?" he asked after she'd calmed down.

"The same," she answered, but her tone said, *Worse*, which made him instantly dizzy. "Your parents' flight landed a little while ago."

"I'll come back."

"I don't know if that's a good idea."

Gilbert was certain it was the *best idea*—the *only* idea.

After the meal and a much-needed toilet break, Gilbert followed Percy to their bedroom. "What's in the bag?" Gilbert dumped most of the contents onto the rug. Percy's eyes went wide, and not only because of the dirt he'd spilled. Curious, they picked through the debris. "Where did you get all this?"

"A long story. Very long."

"It has to do with where you were last night?" Gilbert nodded. "And the tapes?" Gilbert nodded again. "Where are they? Did you still want me to give them a listen?"

"Absolutely no way *in hell*." Pulling out the library book, he said, "But check this out." Gilbert flipped to October's epigraph and read it aloud: *"May these plants find you when you need them most, same as this book."*

They looked up, confused. "I've never heard of these plants. Where did you get them? And this book, for that matter?"

"It's going to sound weird, but . . . I'll try to explain."

While they dug through the tangles of stems, leaves, roots, and petals, Gilbert shared his story. He knew they didn't have much time, so he boiled it down to the most important parts.

Percy believed; the evidence was laid out before them.

Finally, they found a promising passage in October's book. "When crushed with garlic, oil, and the berries of Chimera's Spirit, the Caduceus Flower treats bites and scratches from *Elsewhere* animals." Some of the plants matched the pictures on this page.

Downstairs, they collected other ingredients from the cupboards, along with bowls, measuring cups, and a whisk. Mrs. Scala was folding laundry in the living room, the television blaring. Soon, the two had whipped up an opaque violet liquid the consistency of cough syrup. Percy emptied a glass juice container and poured it in. "What if it's not safe?" they asked.

Gilbert shuddered, unsure. "November's sister helped me find it. From what I heard on those tapes, it's clear they don't see eye to eye. I trust her. *I have to.*"

"What if Mr. November only wants you to think that?"

Gilbert shook his head, not ready for a quarrel. He grabbed his phone from the plug. "We've got to get to the hospital."

"The subway? Again? Now?"

There was so much that Percy didn't understand. Would it be better to go off alone? "What about a taxi?" Gilbert suggested, his face flushed. "I'll pay you back."

When Percy asked their mom, she refused. Instead, Mrs. Scala ordered a car.

As they all zoomed toward the bridge, Gilbert stared out the window, memories of the train ride, of the tales, of the magician whirling through his mind.

Sometimes scary stories were like that. Kept you wondering. *Worrying.*

Every now and again, they'd pass someone on the sidewalk who appeared to be watching them. And a couple times, from the shadows between buildings, large shapes seemed to shift and squirm, as if the door he'd opened by listening to the tapes allowed him to finally notice what had always been here.

The violet liquid sloshed inside the satchel. *Hold on, Ant,* he thought. And then, *Please, let this work.* Deep down, he wondered if this was only a bandage. Gauze and tape. Even if Ant woke up, got all the way better even, what would stop November from coming after them again?

And again?

Until he finally claimed what he wanted?

There had to be an answer . . .

When Grandma Rosemary saw them at the elevator, she looked both gratified and exasperated. Hugs ensued. More scolding too, but that was nothing compared to what Gilbert had already been through.

A moment later, Gilbert and Percy slipped away while the older women commiserated.

Seeing the state of his brother, Gilbert felt a crumpling in his chest. Ant's brown complexion was now grayish, his breathing weak. Beneath the patches of white gauze, dark tendrils branched across his skin. The toxin was spreading.

Percy lifted the oxygen mask away. Moving the bottle toward Ant's lips, Gilbert heard a creaking sound. The bathroom door was opening. Trembling, he nudged it shut with his toe.

Steadying his grip, Gilbert tilted the bottle, the tincture spilling little by little into his brother's slack mouth. Some of it dripped down Ant's chin and soaked his hospital gown. Percy adjusted the angle of Ant's head. The liquid funneled, then trickled down his throat.

"That's all of it," said Gilbert.

"What now?" asked Percy.

BOOM!

The bathroom door hit the wall.

Gilbert spun, his sneakers slipping, and he nearly slumped over onto Ant.

The darkness in the doorway gaped, and something near the toilet stretched what looked like leathery limbs.

"Gilbert?" Percy's voice came out sounding half-crushed.

"Get back," he warned, holding out his arms. The satchel slid from his shoulder and caught in the bend of his elbow. The tapes clacked against the Walkman.

The thing in the bathroom moved toward the light. Gilbert's throat made a clicking noise as he struggled to breathe.

This isn't happening, he thought. *This isn't real.*

But it *was* real.

He knew now because Percy was screaming. "What *is* that?"

Gilbert blinked, tried to process what he was seeing. "It's . . . an *Elsewhere* creature," he stammered. "From one of the tapes. The first story. 'Exterminators.'"

Here were its thin legs.

Its furry body.

Slick black membranes reached out like bat wings.

Then came the quick scrabbling of sharp claws on tile.

Gilbert looked around for a weapon. He grasped the empty bottle like a club.

The creature peeked its dog-like skull through the doorway. Midnight-colored eyes were clumped in the center, reflecting the pale light over Ant's bed. Worst of all was its mouth—a nightmare of spikes and teeth.

Mr. November had known that Gilbert took plants from his garden. He'd known how Gilbert would use them. And he'd sent this monster—the same that had hurt his brother—through the bathroom portal to stop him.

The creature lunged. Gilbert grabbed the door. Swung. The edge caught its spindle legs at the frame. There was a crunch, and a sonic squeal nearly ruptured his eardrums. "Go!" he told Percy. "Hurry!"

"But Ant! We can't leave him."

Gilbert held the door as the thing on the other side battled to free its trapped appendages.

Ant was lying motionless. Had the tonic worked at all? It looked like some color was coming back into his face, but right now wasn't the best time to make judgments. Still, Ant needed time to heal.

Mr. November would have known this, so he was trying to steal the time back from them.

Gilbert stretched for the call button, but it was too far. His fingers only brushed at it. "A little help?"

Percy raced around the bed. Pressed the button. An alarm sounded. Its intermittent chime—*ding-ding-ding*—reminded Gilbert of the subway ride.

"STAND CLEAR OF THE CLOSING DOORS, PLEASE."

No one came. At least not yet. It was a busy unit. But still . . . where were the nurses?

The thing in the bathroom shoved at the door again, forcing its legs farther out, pushing its formidable weight against Gilbert's hold. He felt too weak to keep at it. Even when Percy joined in.

The gap opened wide enough that its head poked through again. Then its shoulders and abdomen. Its jaw, if that's what you could call it, snapped and clicked, and that high-pitched whine vibrated Gilbert's bones. One spindle leg swiped at them, and they had to leap away to avoid its claw. The creature spilled awkwardly through the doorway.

Gilbert grabbed at Percy's arm. They stood frozen, watching for its next move. The thing's eyes shifted toward Ant, still unconscious in the bed, and a thin line of dark saliva dripped to the floor, puddled like spilled ink. It looked ready to pounce. "Hey!" Gilbert shouted, waving. "Over here!" The spidery eyes zeroed in on him. "That's right. Follow us."

Percy understood the unspoken plan. Together they backed toward the light of the hallway, leading the creature away from Ant. All at once, it came for them. In the hall, Gilbert and Percy broke apart, and the thing slammed into the wall. For a moment, it was dazed. The fluorescents seemed to confuse it, blind it almost. This gave Gilbert time to close the door to Ant's room.

Percy yelled for help. But Gilbert knew that no one in the hospital would be able to stop the creature. Not Grandma Rosemary. Not the nurses. Not security. If anyone did end up coming, they might get hurt. They might end up the same as Ant. Or worse.

The glimmer of an idea that had been teasing him all morning began to solidify in his mind.

Stories are doorways to other worlds.

And if stories *could* open these doors, did it mean they might close them too?

By some miracle, the leather satchel was still dangling from Gilbert's arm. He was suddenly certain that the way to stop Mr. November was tucked safely inside.

The creature shook itself out. Its focus was returning.

The important thing was to keep it from Ant. They needed it to follow them. Gilbert also knew he'd require time to accomplish what he now knew he had to do.

And to find that time, they'd need a place to hide.

Gilbert and Percy ran down the hall, not looking back. Claws clickety-clacked as the thing took off after them.

Good. Stay away from my brother.

The first door they came to was marked EMPLOYEES ONLY. The two ducked inside, closed the door, turned the lock. A moment later, this door rattled. Scratching and scrabbling sounds echoed violently on the other side.

The room was small, no larger than an oversize closet.

There was a microwave stand. A coffee maker. A mini fridge. Gilbert and Percy shoved a table and some chairs up against the door, then backed away.

"What do we do?" Percy whispered.

"We lock November out," Gilbert answered, crouching and dumping the contents of the satchel. The cassette cases and the Walkman clattered to the floor.

"How?"

"There's something special about these tapes. About this player. They are what opened the door to . . . Eldritch Place. So they must be what closes it." Gilbert pressed a button on the Walkman he hadn't yet touched: RECORD. "To do that, we tell a new story."

Despite streams of tears and snot, Percy managed a smile. "Where do we start?"

Gilbert thought back to yesterday morning, right before he'd learned how very bad things were about to become.

The tape whirred in the machine. Trying to invoke the tales he'd listened to, he spoke into the microphone, "Gilbert Campbell was shelving books at the public library on the Upper West Side when his phone dinged . . ."

The scratching at the door became a pounding, so hard that the table and chairs stacked before it began to tremble. This didn't sound like the creature anymore, but like fists. A voice rose up, called through the door. "Stop this now!" It was like the voice from the red phone, in the tale about the ice cream truck. The one that had threatened Dagmar. Low and rich, like a stringed instrument. "This is your final warning."

As it spoke, Gilbert felt a sensation like nothing he'd ever experienced. As if . . . his bones were shivering. There was no time to get through the entire story. Of the train and the tapes. Gilbert needed to skip to the ending. "Mr. November was not as strong as he believed," he said. The shriek that followed was midnight and poison and fangs and acid. The farthest parts of the unknown. Swirling mists and the spirals of seashells. Black holes and supernovas. "Gilbert and Percy knew they could defeat him."

"Yeah!" Percy chimed in.

"If stories open doorways to other worlds," said Gilbert, "they can close them too."

He went on, telling the tale of how he and Percy had barricaded themselves in a break room at the hospital. How the pounding at the door was growing weaker. How November's portal from his Eldritch Place home was disappearing. That, one by one, *all* of his doors were going away.

The voice boomed from the hallway again: "You have no idea what I've learned. You have no idea *what I am*. But you're about to find out . . ."

"Gilbert, look!" Percy pointed.

Beyond the stacked table and chairs, the wooden door looked like it was disintegrating, the wood grain being eaten to bits. On the other side, they could now see a tall figure, nothing like the man Gilbert had met in the house with the garden. This one was dressed in black—an old-fashioned suit, a high-collared cape latched at the throat, a top hat tilted jauntily upon a bald skull. The gaunt face looked barely human. Black holes peered from where eyes should have been, skin stretched too tight, a sliver of a mouth twisted into a sneer. November's mask was stripped away, the veil pulled aside. He spoke with the voice of a coming storm: *"How . . . dare . . . you!"*

He raised pale hands—fingers blackened, nails long and jagged—toward Gilbert and Percy to clutch and squeeze and *punish*. He waved one of them. The table and chairs flew aside, smashed against the wall. Then he stepped inside.

Gilbert's own voice was drying up, but he managed to spit out his ending. "Gilbert and Percy laughed as the passage crumbled, trapping November outside of their world forever and ever."

In an instant, the figure dissolved like salt in water and was gone.

The tape hissed and hissed and hissed.

Then, silence.

GILBERT AT THE DOOR

By the end of April, Percy's plants had started to grow. Green peeped from the ground, and in a few spots, flowers were blooming. Yellows and pinks and purples and reds. They'd used the seeds and root bulbs that Gilbert had taken from the magician's front yard and mixed them into the small garden behind the Scalas' rowhouse.

Every day, Gilbert looked forward to seeing the changes.

He knelt by one of the flowerbeds. The new sprouts looked ordinary enough, but he understood that what made them different was hidden—underground or within. *Give them a few months*, Gilbert thought, *and they'll make themselves known.* Using a trowel, he spread some mulch.

"Missed a spot," said Percy, nudging the bag toward him.

"I'm getting there," Gilbert answered, flicking a bit of dirt. "Hold your ponies!"

Percy laughed.

Something moved through the soil, just beneath the surface. Both kids shifted onto their heels. After a few seconds, Gilbert exhaled. Percy tossed him a worried look, but he shook his head. "It's fine," Gilbert added. According to the book by October Bowen, planting seeds and bulbs and cuttings from *Elsewhere* tended to attract the creatures that knew them, those visitors who'd snuck through strange gaps like the one November's tapes had opened.

Still, Percy worried that these new visitors were not in fact harmless.

In his heart, Gilbert knew that growing these plants was necessary. Look what they'd done for his brother . . .

When Ant had finally been well enough to leave the hospital, Gilbert looked into replacing Mrs. Effiong's copy of *Elsewhere Gardens*. The book had come to him when he'd needed it, like October Bowen had written in the epigraph. Unsurprisingly, there were no copies available online. Gilbert felt bad about keeping it, but not *too* bad. His parents ordered a different botany book for the library instead.

What gave him hope was seeing how different October's kind of magic was from her brother's. *December is darkness. November is what's coming. October is the magic that prepares you for the other two.*

Now Ant was almost fully recovered. Though his scars were growing fainter, he sometimes complained of headaches as well as shortness of breath.

He claimed to not remember what had happened, not even when Gilbert had played back his own garbled voice message. *"Don't listen to the tapes . . ."* If Ant was telling the truth—*was he?*—maybe not remembering was for the best.

Sometimes, Gilbert hoped he'd forget the tales himself. He still woke in the dark, nightmare images lingering in the shadows of his bedroom—squirming tentacles, needle-teeth, robotic hands, skulls with eye sockets like black holes. But if he forgot the tales, *the tapes*, then he might forget the recording he'd made with Percy in the break room at the hospital.

He understood *that* particular tale might be the one thing holding November at bay.

In the past few weeks, shadows had stuck in the corners of his vision, as if waiting for Gilbert to turn his head so they could grab at him. Since the stories had remained in his mind, some of their details were still visible in the real world.

If he could see them, could they see him? Like peeking through a window?

Gilbert worried that November or one of his minions might find a way to steal the tape, unspool it, or worse.

Keeping it safe was imperative.

"*You have reached your destination . . .*" The words from his dad's GPS gave Gilbert shivers. The destination in question happened to be a small town several hours north of the city.

About a week ago, Percy had located an esoteric shop called the Elsewhere Bazaar. Its website stated that the name of its proprietress was O. Bowen. When Gilbert had called the phone number, a young woman answered. "Is this October?" he'd asked, trying to keep his voice from trembling.

"No, sorry. Ms. Bowen isn't in the shop today. Maybe I can help? My name's Amelia. I'm her assistant." Amelia told him that her boss was slightly frail, so she usually only came to the shop on weekends.

It didn't take much to convince his parents. "Couldn't we all use a break?" Gilbert had asked. "Together?"

His father parked on a village street. Gilbert crawled from the back seat with Percy and Ant, who yawned and stretched and looked around with curiosity. They'd asked Grandma Rosemary to come along too, but she hated long rides.

There were quaint cafés, antique shops, galleries, and a couple bookstores. A blue silhouette of mountains rolled along the horizon. From down the hill, you could hear the faint hush of a creek and a waterfall.

The city was a world away.

"Who's hungry?" Gilbert's mother asked.

"I could eat," answered his dad.

"Me too," said Ant.

Gilbert and Percy simply glanced at each other. They'd already noticed the bazaar's sign hanging out over the sidewalk. "Can we stop here first?" Gilbert asked.

"We'll meet you there," said Mom, peering into an antique shop. "I want to ask about this cute table first." She grabbed Dad's hand and headed inside.

Ant looked suspicious. "You good?" he asked.

"We're good," Gilbert answered, really meaning it.

Ant shrugged and then followed his parents.

Gilbert slung the leather satchel up his shoulder and clasped the strap tightly, as if someone might swipe it. The tape was inside. He'd brought it all this way, hoping that October Bowen—the author who'd saved them once before—might agree to protect the tale from her estranged brother.

Gilbert stood with Percy at the entry to the Elsewhere Bazaar, staring at himself in the window's reflection. Inside, he made out tables stuffed with herb jars and vases of cut flowers. There were books and statues and bins with metal scoops attached by thin chains. In a far corner . . . Was that a seashell? With spikes?

A stooped and elderly woman was organizing crowded shelves. Her alabaster mane was fine, gathered back into an unusually long ponytail. Helping her was a girl with pale skin and dark hair, who looked maybe a few years older than himself. Was this Amelia? October's assistant?

There was a tug at his sleeve. "Do you see that?" Percy sounded scared.

In the reflection, a man stood behind them, far back across the street. He wore an old-fashioned suit with a high-collared cape, latched at the throat. His top hat tilted jauntily upon his bald skull. Black holes peered from where eyes should have been, skin stretched too tight, a sliver of a mouth twisted into a sneer.

Before Gilbert could gasp, the man rushed them, footfalls smacking against asphalt, arms reaching, fingertips blackened. His mouth stretched wide, and a voice boomed in Gilbert's head.

How . . . dare . . . you!

Spinning, he found the street empty, except for a passing car.

"Come on, Gilbert," said Percy, grabbing the handle and swinging open the shop's door.

A bell chimed.

They both stepped through.

"The boss said I could pick these," Gilbert mentioned.

Clay glanced sideways through the screen door.

Gilbert opened the satchel and grabbed at the plants, snapping stems, pulling up roots, plucking various blossoms as quickly as he could, shoving them all inside. A bittersweet aroma filled the air—dirt and loam and minerals stirred up from the ground.

"Hey!" Clay shouted. "Stop that."

Gilbert dashed through the emerald trellis to the subway steps.

Down, down, down.

Heavy now, the leather satchel bounced against his ribs.

Footfalls echoed from the corridor behind him.

At the platform, Gilbert raced toward the parked train and swung around the edge of an open doorway, slamming into the seat and scrunching his legs up to his chest. He squeezed his eyes shut, as if that would make him invisible.

In a moment, Clay would find him, rip the satchel away—

"STAND CLEAR OF THE CLOSING DOORS, PLEASE," said the happy voice from the speakers. Chimes rang, and the doors slid shut.

As the train trembled to life, Gilbert glanced out the window, caught a glimpse of shadow descending the steps. By then, the train was speeding up, delivering him from Aldridge Place.

Before the car slipped into darkness, he watched the tiles

that spelled out the station's name flicker, transform, revealing a different name entirely—*Eldritch Place*—confirming his fear that everything he'd seen here had been an illusion, a lie . . .

A story.

ACKNOWLEDGMENTS

I speak countless thanks into the VOID for the many magicians (secret, and not so secret) who assisted in making *more* of these tales: Alex Wolfe, Rob Valois, Caroline Press, Mary Claire Cruz, Araselly Rodriguez, Karter Powell, Trevor Ingerson, Shara Hardeson, Danielle Colburn, and the whole team at Penguin Workshop. To Marie Bergeron. To Vivian Kirklin and Ana Deboo. To Ben Estes. To Michael Bourret and the crew at DG&B. To Bethany Ides, Ora Ferdman, Matthew Sawicki, Jan Niemira, Nick Cramer, and Brad Crater. To Ellen Oh, Daniel Kraus, and Kate Alice Marshall. You all know what you did . . . and I hope you know how much I appreciate you.